ONCE UPON THE RIVER LOVE

Also by Andreï Makine

A Hero's Daughter

Confessions of a Fallen Standard-Bearer

The Earth and Sky of Jacques Dorme

Dreams of My Russian Summers

The Crime of Olga Arbyelina

Requiem for a Lost Empire

Music of a Life

The Woman Who Waited

ONCE UPON THE RIVER LOVE

A NOVEL

ANDREÏ MAKINE

Translated from the French by
Geoffrey Strachan

ARCADE PUBLISHING • NEW YORK

Originally published in French under the title *Au temps du fleuve Amour*

Visit our website at www.arcadepub.com.

10 9 8 7 6 5 4 3 2 1

Library of Congress Cataloging-in-Publication Data is available on file.

ISBN: 978-1-61145-806-0

Printed in the United States of America

for D.A.

Translator's Note

ANDREÏ MAKINE WAS BORN and brought up in Russia but wrote *Once Upon the River Love* in French, while living in France. Much of the novel is set in eastern Siberia, close to the mighty river Amur — the frontier between Siberia and Manchuria. But Amur is also one of the Russian names for Cupid, the god of love, and in French the name of the river is spelled Amour, the French for "love." The French title of Makine's novel, *Au Temps du Fleuve Amour,* thus contains a play on words in French and Russian that cannot be captured precisely in English, hence the title that has been given to this translation.

In his French text, Makine uses a number of Russian words for basic features of Siberian and Soviet life. I have generally left these as English transliterations of Russian. These include: *izba* (a traditional wooden house built of logs); *shapka* (a fur hat or cap, often with earflaps); *taiga* (the virgin pine forest that spreads across Siberia south of the tundra); *kolkhoz* (a collective farm); *kolkhoznik* (a worker on such a farm); *muzhik* (the somewhat contemptuous historic word for a peasant); *kulak* (a peasant farmer, working for his own profit); *apparatchik* (a member of the Communist Party or government apparatus).

≋ 1 ≋

≈ 1 ≈

HER BODY IS A softened, glowing crystal on a glassblower's pipe. . . .

Can you hear me clearly, Utkin? Under your fevered pen, the woman I'm telling you about in our transatlantic conversation tonight will flower. Her body, this glass with the hot brilliance of a ruby, will become a softer color. Her breasts will become firmer, turning a milky pink. Her thighs will bear a swarm of beauty spots — the hallmarks of your impatient fingers. . . .

Speak of her, Utkin!

The closeness of the sea can be guessed at from the light on the ceiling. It is still too hot to go down to the beach. Everything is drowsing in this great house lost amid the greenery: a broad-brimmed straw hat, glowing in the sunlight on the terrace; in the garden, twisted cherry trees with motionless branches and trunks oozing resin. And then this newspaper, several weeks old, with its columns that carry news of the ending of our distant empire. And the sea, a turquoise incrustation between the branches of the cherry trees . . . I am stretched out in a room that seems to be tilting across the great glassy bay with its sparkling expanse of sea. All is white, all is sunlight. Apart from the great black stain of the piano, a refugee from rainy evenings. And in an armchair: *she*. Still a little distant — we have known each other only two weeks. A few swims together in the foam; a few evening strolls in the fragrant shade of the cypress trees. A few kisses. She's a princess of the blood — just imagine, Utkin! Even if she is royally indifferent to the fact. I am her bear, her barbarian, all the way from the land of everlasting snows. An ogre! This amuses her. . . .

At this moment she is bored with the long wait of the afternoon. She gets up, crosses to the piano, opens the lid. The slow notes stir as if unwillingly, quiver like butterflies whose wings are weighed down with pollen, and sink into the sun-drenched silence of the empty building. . . .

I stand up in my turn. With the litheness of a wild animal. I am quite naked. Does she sense me drawing close? She does not even turn her head when I embrace her hips. She continues to plunge her long, lazy notes into the air liquefied by the heat.

She pauses and cries out only when she suddenly feels me inside her. And seeking to recover her balance, overtaken by a joyful delirium, she leans on the piano, no longer looking at the keys. With both hands. Her fingers fanned out. A thunderous drunken major chord erupts. And the wild sounds coincide with her first moans. As I penetrate her, I push her, I lift her, I take her weight. Her only point of support is her hands, moving on the keyboard once more. . . . A chord noisier and still more insistent. She is all curved now, her head thrown back, the lower part of her body abandoned to me. Yes, trembling, rippling, like a red-hot mass on a glassblower's pipe. The beads of sweat make this oval of flesh swaying beneath my fingers quite transparent. . . .

And the chords follow one another, more and more staccato, breathless. And her cries answer them in a deafening symphony of pleasure: sunlight, the clangor of the chords, the loud outbursts of her voice, mingling happy sobs with cries of fury. And when she feels me exploding inside her, the symphony breaks up into a stream of shrill and feverish notes, bursting forth beneath her fingers. Her hands drum furiously as she clings to the smooth keys. As if they were clinging to the invisible edge of the pleasure that is already slipping away from her body . . .

And in this silence, still throbbing with a thousand echoes, I can see her glowing transparent form slowly suffused with the bronzed opacity of repose. . . .

Utkin calls that "raw material." One day he telephoned me from New York and asked me, in a slightly bashful voice, to tell him in a letter about one of my adventures. "Don't polish it," he warned me. "In any case I'll change everything around. . . . What interests me is the raw material."

Utkin writes. He has always dreamed of writing. Even when we were boys in the depths of eastern Siberia. But he lacks subject matter. With his lame leg and his shoulder that sticks up at an acute angle, he has never had any luck in love. This tragic paradox has tortured him since his childhood: why was he the one to be catapulted under blocks of ice in the frenzied breakup of a great river, which crushed his body and then spewed it out, irremediably mutilated? While the other one, myself . . . And I would murmur the name of the river — Amur — that bears the same name as the god of love, and enter into its cool resonance, as if into the body of a woman in a dream, one created from similar matter, supple, soft, and misty.

All that is long ago now. Utkin writes. He asks me not to polish. I understand him; he wants to be the sole architect. He wants to outwit blind fate. And as for the sea's turquoise incrustations between the branches of the cherry trees — it is he who will add them to my story. I do not make refinements. I present him with my mass of red-hot glass just as it is. I do not engrave it with the point of my chisel or inflate it with my breath. Just as it is: a young woman with a bronzed back, a woman crying out, sobbing with pleasure and beating the clusters of her fingers against the keys of the piano . . .

2

BEAUTY WAS THE least of our preoccupations in the land where we were born, Utkin, me, and the others. You could spend your whole life there and never discover whether you were ugly or beautiful, never seek out the secrets of the mosaic of the human face or the mystery of the sensual topography of the human body.

Love, too, did not easily take root in this austere country. Love for love's sake had, I think, simply been forgotten — had atrophied in the bloodbath of the war, been garroted by the barbed-wire entanglements of the nearby camp, frozen by the breath of the Arctic. And if love survived, it took only one form, that of love-as-sin. Always more or less fictitious, it brightened up the routine of harsh winter days. Women muffled up in several shawls would stop in the middle of the village and pass on the exciting news. They believed they were whispering, but because of their shawls they were obliged to shout. And our young ears would pick up the secret being divulged. On this occasion the headmistress of the school had apparently been seen in the cabin of a refrigerator truck. . . . Yes, you know, those broad cabins with a little berth behind them. And the truck had been parked just by the Devil's Bend, yes, the very place where a truck overturns at least once a year. It was impossible to imagine the headmistress, a curt woman of an improbable age, who wore a whole carapace of flannelette-lined garments, romping in the arms of a truckdriver who smelled of cedar resin, tobacco, and gasoline. Especially at the Devil's Bend. But this fantasy of copulation in a cabin with frosted-up windows released little fizzing bubbles into the icy air of the village. The parade of indignation warmed their chilled hearts. And people almost resented the headmistress for not being seen scrambling up into every truck carrying the trunks of huge pine trees through the taiga. . . . The stir aroused by this latest piece of tittle-tattle quickly faded away, as if congealed under the icy wind of endless nights. In our eyes the headmistress became once more as everyone knew her: a woman irremediably alone and resigned to her misery. And the trucks roared by as usual, obsessed with transporting the number of cubic meters of load specified in the plan. The taiga closed in on the brilliance of their headlights. The white breath of the women's voices dissolved in the biting wind. And the village, sobered up from its erotic fantasies, huddled up and settled into the eternity known as "winter."

From the time of its birth, the village was not conceived as a haven for love. The czar's cossacks, who had founded it three centuries earlier, never even thought about it. They were a handful of men overwhelmed with fatigue from their crazy trek into the depths of the endless taiga. The haughty stares of the wolves followed them even into their turbulent dreams. The cold was quite different from that in Russia. It seemed to know no limits. Covered with thick hoarfrost, their beards stood out like ax blades. And if you closed your eyes for a moment, your lashes would not come unstuck. The cossacks cursed in vexation and despair. And their spit tinkled as it fell in little lumps of ice on the dark surface of a motionless river.

Of course, they too experienced love on occasion. There were these women with slanting eyes and impassive faces that seemed as if haunted by mysterious smiles. The cossacks made love to them on bearskins in the smoky darkness of yurts, beside the glowing embers. But the bodies of these taciturn lovers were passing strange. Anointed with reindeer fat, their bodies slipped from your grasp. To hold on to them, you had to twist their long glistening tresses, as black and coarse as a horse's mane, around your fist. Their breasts were flat and round, like the domes of the oldest churches in Kiev, and their hips were firm and resistant. But once tamed by the hand holding back their manes, their bodies no longer slipped away. Their eyes blazed like the cutting edges of sabers, their lips grew rounded, ready to bite. And the scent of their skin, tanned by the fire and the cold, became more and more pungent, intoxicating. And this intoxication did not fade away. . . . The cossack would wind the tresses around his fist a second time. And in the narrow eyes of the woman there flashed a spark of mischief. Has he not drunk a draft of that viscous, brownish infusion — the blood of the Kharg root — which floods your veins with the power of all your ancestors?

Breaking the spell, the cossack would go back to his companions, and for several more days he would be impervious to the bite of the cold. The Kharg root was singing in his veins.

Their goal was always that improbable Far East with its thrilling promise of the land's end: the great misty void, so dear to their souls, that detested constraints, limits, frontiers. In the west, when it had conclusively driven back barbarian Muscovy, Europe had established a line that could not be crossed. And so they had gone headlong toward the east. Hoping to reach the Western World from the other end? The ruse of a neglected admirer? The ploy of a banished lover?

Most of all, though, they were venturers into the misty void. To stop at the land's end in the warm spring dusk and to let their gaze soar up from that ultimate brink toward the shy pallor of the first stars . . .

After several months, their numbers much reduced since the start, they finally halted, on this extremity of their native Eurasia. There, where the earth, the sky, and the ocean are one . . . And in a smoke-filled yurt, in the heart of the taiga, where winter still reigned, a woman, whose snake body was horribly distorted, writhed as she expelled an extraordinarily large infant onto a bear-skin. He had slanting eyes like his mother, and prominent cheek-bones like all his kinsmen. But his damp hair glistened. A flash of dark gold.

And the people thronged around the young mother in silent contemplation of this new Siberian.

What had come down to us of this mythical past was but a remote legend. An echo muted by the confused hubbub of the centuries. In our imaginations the cossacks had still not finished hacking a route for themselves through the virgin taiga. And a young Yakut girl, clad in a short sable coat, was forever rummaging in the tangle of stems and branches in search of the famous Kharg root. . . . It was surely no coincidence if the power that dreams, songs, and legends had over our barbarian hearts was irresistible. Our own life was turning into a dream!

And yet in our day all that was left of this memory of the centuries was a heap of worm-eaten wood on top of granite blocks covered in lichen. The ruins of the church built by the descendants of the cossacks and dynamited during the Revolution. Or elsewhere rusty nails, as thick as a man's thumb, driven into the trunks of huge cedar trees. Even the old people of the village retained only a very vague memory of these: sometimes it was the Whites who had brutally executed a group of partisans by having them hanged from these nails; sometimes it was the Reds who had meted out revolutionary justice. . . . The nails, and the bits of rotted rope, had risen, over long years, to twice a man's height, in accordance with the slow and stately growth of the cedars. To our marveling eyes the Reds and the Whites, who had gone in for these cruel hangings, had the stature of giants. . . .

The village had not contrived to preserve anything of its past. From the start of the century, history, like a titanic pendulum, had begun to sweep fearsomely to and fro across the empire. The men went away; the women dressed in black. The pendulum kept the measure of passing time: the war against Japan; the war against Germany; the Revolution; the civil war. . . . And then once again, but in reverse order: the war against the Germans; the war against the Japanese. And the men went away, now crossing the twelve thousand leagues of the empire to fill the trenches in the west, now disappearing into the misty void of the ocean to the east. The pendulum swung westward, and the Whites drove the Reds back beyond the Urals, beyond the Volga. Its weight returned, sweeping across Siberia: now the Reds drove the Whites back toward the Far East. They hammered nails into the trunks of cedar trees and dynamited churches — as if all the better to assist the pendulum in wiping out every trace of the past.

One day the mighty swing even catapulted men from our own village toward that fabled Western World that had long since marked itself off from barbaric Muscovy. From the Volga they traveled as far as Berlin, paving the route with their corpses. There in Berlin the crazy clock stopped for an instant — a short moment of victory. Then the survivors returned toward the east: now accounts had to be settled with Japan. . . .

Ever since our childhood, however, the pendulum seemed to have stuck. It was as if its immense weight had become entangled in the innumerable lines of barbed-wire fencing stretched across its path. Indeed, there was a camp about a dozen miles from our village. There was a place on the road leading to the town where the taiga opened up and in the cold glitter of the fog you could see the silhouettes of the watchtowers. How many of these snares strewn across the empire did the pendulum encounter as it swung? God alone knows.

The village, depopulated, did not amount to more than a score of izbas. There, close by that pent-up mass of human lives, it seemed to be asleep. The camp, a black speck amid the endless snows . . .

A child needs very little in order to construct its personal universe: a few natural landmarks whose harmony it can readily uncover and which it arranges into a coherent world. It was thus that the microcosm of our young years organized itself. We knew the place in a deep thicket in the taiga where a stream arose, emerging from the dark mirror of an underground wellspring. This stream — the Brook as everyone called it — circled the village and flowed into the river near the abandoned bathhouse: a river that wound its way between two dark walls of the taiga, wide and deep. It had a proper name, Olyei, and figured in a broader geographical role, since the direction in which it flowed marked the north-south line, and a long way from the village it met up with a mighty river: the river Amur. This was marked on the dusty globe that our old geography teacher occasionally showed to us. In our primitive microcosm, the human habitations were also arranged according to this hierarchy of three levels: our village, Svetlaya; then, six miles from the village, farther downstream on the Olyei, Kazhdai, a district center; and finally, on the great river itself, the only real city,

Nerlug, which had a store where you could even buy lemonade in bottles. . . .

The upheavals caused by the pendulum had made the population of the village very motley, despite the primitive simplicity of its existence. Among us there was a former "kulak," exiled here during the collectivization of the Ukraine in the thirties; a family of old believers, the Klestovs, who lived in fierce isolation, hardly talking to anyone else; and a ferryman, Verbin, who had only one arm and who always told the same story to his passengers. He was one of the first to have inscribed his name on the walls of the conquered Reichstag; and it was at that ecstatic moment of victory that a stray shell splinter had severed his right arm — when he was only halfway through his name!

The pendulum had also crushed families. There were hardly any complete ones apart from that of the old believers. My friend Utkin lived with his mother, alone. As long as he was a child and could not understand, she would tell him that his father had been a pilot in the war and that he had perished in a kamikaze attack, hurling his blazing plane at a column of German tanks. But one day Utkin had realized that since he was born twelve years after the war, it was physically impossible for him to have had such a father. Mortified, he said this to his mother. She explained, blushing, that it had been the Korean War. . . . Fortunately, there was no shortage of wars.

As for myself, I had only my aunt. . . . The pendulum in its flight must have scraped the frozen soil of our land and uncovered rivers with golden sand. Or perhaps some of the gilding on its heavy disk had rubbed off on the rough earth. . . . My aunt had no need to invent aeronautical exploits. My father, a geologist, had followed the pendulum's gilded trail. He must secretly have hoped to discover some new gold-bearing terrain for the day of my birth. His body was never found. And my mother died in labor. . . .

As for Samurai, who was fifteen at this time, neither Utkin nor I could ever properly understand who the hook-nosed old woman was in whose izba he lived. His mother? His grandmother? He always called her by her first name and cut short all our attempts to learn anything more about her.

The pendulum stopped swinging. And the life of the village was gradually reduced to three essential matters: timber, gold, and the chill shadow of the camp. It was beyond us to imagine our futures unfolding outside these three prime elements. One day, we thought, we would have to join the men who disappeared into the taiga with their toothed chain saws. Some of these loggers had come to our icy hell in pursuit of the "northern bonus," the premium that doubled their meager wages. Others — prisoners on parole on condition of good work and exemplary conduct — counted not rubles but days. . . . Or perhaps we would be among those gold prospectors we sometimes saw coming into the workers' canteen: huge fox-fur shapkas; short fur coats, held in with broad belts; gigantic boots lined with smooth, glistening fur. It was said that among them were some who "stole gold from the state." Yes, they washed sand on unknown terrains and disposed of their nuggets on a mysterious "black market." As children, we were certainly much tempted by such a future.

There was one more choice open to us: to freeze there in the chill shadow, aiming an automatic rifle from the top of a watchtower at the ranks of prisoners drawn up beside their huts. Or ourselves disappear into the seething humanity of those barrack huts . . .

All the latest news in Svetlaya revolved around those three elements: taiga, gold, shadow. We would learn that once again a gang of loggers had disturbed a bear in its lair and escaped by piling, all six of them, into the cabin of their tractor. There was talk of the record weight of a gold nugget "as big as your fist." And there were whispers of yet another escapee. . . . Then came the season of violent snowstorms, and even this thin trickle of information was interrupted. Now the talk was of strictly local news: an electric cable that had snapped, traces of wolves found near the barn. Finally, one day, the village did not wake up. . . .

The villagers got up, prepared breakfast. And suddenly they surprised a strange silence reigning around their izbas. No crunch of footsteps in the snow, no wind whistling around the roof edges, no dogs barking. Nothing. A cotton-wool silence, opaque, absolute. This deaf outside world filtered out all the household sounds that normally went unnoticed. You could hear the sighing of a kettle on the stove, the slight, regular hiss of a lightbulb. We listened, my aunt and I, to the unfathomable depth of this silence. We looked at the clock with its weights. Normally the day should have dawned by then. With our foreheads pressed against the windowpane, we peered into the darkness. The window was completely blocked by snow. Then we rushed to the entrance hall and, already anticipating the unimaginable, which recurred almost every winter, we opened the door. . . .

A wall of snow rose on the threshold of our izba. The village was entirely buried.

With a yell of wild joy, I seized hold of a shovel. No school! No homework! A day of happy chaos awaited us.

I began by digging out a narrow section; then, by packing down the light and feathery snow, I fashioned steps. From time to time my aunt sprinkled the depths of my cavern with hot water from the kettle to ease my task. I was climbing up slowly, compelled at times to proceed almost horizontally. My aunt encouraged me from the threshold of the izba, begging me not to go too fast. I was beginning to be short of breath, I experienced a strange giddiness, my bare hands were burning, my pulse was throbbing heavily in my temples. The light of the dim bulb coming from the izba now scarcely reached the corner where I was hacking away.

Dripping with sweat, despite the snow that surrounded me, I felt as if I were within warm and protective entrails. My body seemed to have memories of prenatal darkness. My brain, dulled by the lack of air, feebly suggested to me that it might have been sensible to go back down into the izba to recover my breath. . . .

It was at that moment that my head pierced the crusty surface of the snow! I closed my eyes; the light was blinding.

Infinite calm reigned over the sun-drenched plain: the serenity of nature at rest after the turmoil of the night. Now the blue distances of the taiga were clearly revealed: it seemed to be asleep in the sweet air. And above the glittering expanse, white columns of smoke arose from invisible chimneys.

The first men appeared, emerging from the snow, and stood up. With dazed looks they took in the glittering desert now spread out where the village had been. Laughing, we hugged one another, pointing at the smoke — it was really comic to picture somebody cooking a meal under six feet of snow! A dog bounded out of the tunnel and seemed to be equally bemused by the unaccustomed spectacle. . . . I saw Klestov, the old believer, appearing. He turned toward the east, crossed himself slowly, then greeted everyone with an air of exaggerated dignity.

Little by little the village rediscovered its familiar sounds. The few men of Svetlaya, helped by all the rest of us, began to dig corridors linking the izbas with one another and opened up the path to the well.

We knew that this abundance of snow in our country of dry cold had been brought by winds that blew from the misty void of the ocean. We also knew that the storm had been the very first sign of spring. The sunlight of this mild spell would soon beat down the snow, would reduce it to heavy piles below our windows. And the cold weather would begin again, even more extreme, as if to take revenge on this brief interval of light abandon. But spring would come! We were sure of it now. A spring as brilliant and sudden as the light that had blinded us as we emerged from our tunnels.

And spring did come: one fine day the village broke its moorings. Our river began to move. Vast acres of ice began their stately procession. Their progress grew faster; the glittering layers of water dazzled us. The raw smell of the ice mingled with the wind from the steppes. And the earth slipped away under our feet. And it was our village, with its izbas, its worm-eaten fences, its sails of multicolored linen on the lines, it was Svetlaya that was embarking on a joyful cruise.

The eternity of winter was coming to an end.

The voyage did not last long. A few weeks later the river returned to its bed and the village landed on the shores of a fleeting Siberian summer. And during this brief interlude the sun spilled out the warm scent of cedar resin. We talked of nothing now but the taiga.

It was in the course of one of our expeditions into the heart of the taiga that Utkin discovered the Kharg root. . . .

With his lame leg, he always lagged behind us. From time to time he would call out to Samurai and me: "Hey, wait up!" Understandingly we would slacken our pace.

This time instead of his usual "Wait up!" he gave a long whistle of surprise. We turned back.

How could he have unearthed it, this root that only the expert eyes of the Yakut women could manage to detect in the soft layer of the humus? Maybe thanks to his leg. His left foot, which he dragged along like a rake, dug up extraordinary things, often without his being aware of it. . . .

We looked closely at the Kharg root. Without admitting it to ourselves, we sensed that there was something feminine about its shape. It was, in fact, a kind of plump, dark-hued pear, with a skin like suede, slightly cracked, the underside was covered in purplish down. From top to bottom the root was divided by a groove that resembled the line of a vertebral column.

The Kharg was very pleasant to touch. Its velvety skin seemed to respond to contact with the fingers. This bulb with its sensual contours hinted at a strange life that animated its mysterious interior.

Intrigued by its secret, I made a scratch on its chubby surface with my thumbnail. A blood-red liquid poured into the scratch mark. We exchanged puzzled looks. "Let me see," demanded Samurai, taking the Kharg from my hands.

He produced his knife and cut into the bulb of the root of love, following the groove. Then, thrusting his thumbs into the down at the base of the fleshy oval, he pulled them apart smartly.

We heard a kind of brief creak — like the sound of a door frozen fast with ice when it finally yields under pressure.

We all bent forward to get a better view. Within a pinkish fleshy lap we saw a long, pale leaf. It was curled up with that moving delicacy often encountered in nature. And it inspired mixed feelings in us: to destroy, to smash this useless harmony, or . . . We really did not know what should be done with it. And thus for several moments we gazed at the leaf; it was reminiscent of the transparency and fragility of the wings of a butterfly emerging from its chrysalis.

Even Samurai seemed vaguely embarrassed, faced with this unexpected and disconcerting beauty.

Finally, with a brisk movement, he stuck the two halves of the Kharg together and thrust the root into a pocket of his knapsack.

"I'll ask Olga," he called out to us as he moved off. "She must have heard of it. . . ."

3

WE LIVED IN A strange universe, without women. The discovery of the bulb of love simply brought this reality out into the open.

Yes, there were a few shadowy figures who were often dear to us; we were fond of them. But for us they had no feminine aura. My aunt; Utkin's mother; old Olga . . . Some of the faces of the women teachers at the school located at Kazhdai. Their femininity had long since been eroded in the harsh business of daily resisting the cold, the solitude, the absence of any foreseeable change. No, they were not ugly. Utkin's mother, for example, had a fine pale face, with a kind of ethereal transparency in her features. But did she know this herself? It is only long afterward, seeing her again in my memory, that I have been able to perceive this: yes, she could have been attractive, desirable. But attractive to whom? Desirable where? Cold, darkness, the eternity known as "winter". . . And the pendulum had gone to sleep, enmeshed in the ice-covered barbed wire.

It happened that, owing to the chance of some allocation decided a thousand leagues from our village, a young woman teacher found herself at our school. A rare commodity. A figure who became the focus of intense curiosity. But we detected such anguish on her face, such a desire to escape as quickly as possible, that we ourselves were made uneasy by it: was our life really so unbearable? Her anguish distorted her features. Her beauty, her fascinating strangeness, became blurred beneath this grimace of terror. We all felt that she was mentally counting the days — she looked at us as if we were already in the past. People who figured in an unhappy memory. Characters in a nightmare.

And the men, in thrall to those three elements — taiga, gold, and the shadow of the watchtowers — were doing their counting as well . . . in cubic meters of cedarwood or kilograms of gold-bearing sand. They, too, dreamed of a completely different existence, when all this counting was over; of a life ten thousand leagues distant from this country — beyond the Urals, at the other end of the empire. They would mention the Ukraine, the Caucasus, the Crimea. As their saws bit into the aromatic flesh of the cedar trees, they seemed to be shrieking: "Crrr-i-mea," out of yearning for it. And the dredging machines of the gold prospectors echoed them as they dug: "Crrr-i-mea."

And as for love . . . The only word we ever heard them use was "have." Not "have a night with," which might have evoked the occasion. Still less "have an affair"; that might even have suggested a process of seduction; but simply "have a woman." Lurking in a corner of the workers' canteen, behind our glasses of stewed fruit, we listened to them exchanging secrets and were always desperately disappointed by them. Their stories only told us of one thing: that one of them had "had" an unknown woman. No backdrops, no portraits, no erotic imagery. They did not even bother trying to characterize their exploits by using one of the obscene verbs that regularly reverberated in their throats, burned with vodka and the wind.

"Huh! I've had her, that little Yakut. . . ."

"You know that Maria on the cash till? I've had her."

We hoped at least for some details: What was she like, that young Yakut woman? Beneath her fur coat hardened by the fierce hoarfrosts, her body must have seemed particularly warm and smooth. And her hair must have had the scent of cedar smoke; and her strong, slightly curved legs and her muscular thighs doubtless made her groin a veritable trap that closed in on her lover's body. . . . We awaited just one of these revelations so feverishly! But the men had already started talking about cubic meters of wood, or a tube that needed to be extended so that the nuggets could be dislodged more readily. . . . We swallowed the soft fruits in our stew noisily, we cracked the apricot stones with the heavy handles of our knives. And chewing on the kernels, we went out into the icy wind, with a bitter taste on our lips.

Love seemed to us to be something carved from the gray dusk of a dreary district center, where all the streets led out into wastelands covered by wet sawdust.

And then one day we had this encounter in the heart of the taiga. It was the same summer that Utkin's injured foot had unearthed the love root. I was just fourteen, and I still did not know whether I was ugly or handsome, or whether there was any more to love than "I've had her."

On the bank of a river, on a hot August afternoon, we had lit a wood fire. Casting off our clothes, we hurled ourselves into the water. Despite the sun, it was icy cold. A few moments later we were already warming ourselves by the fire. Then once more a dive and quickly the burning caress of the flames. It was the only way to spend all day in the water. Utkin — he never bathed because of his leg — kept the fire going, and we two, Samurai and I, stark naked, would pit ourselves against the rapid current of the Olyei. Then, our teeth chattering, we rushed back toward the fire, jostling each other but never forgetting to bring a little water in the hollow of our palms. We hurled it at Utkin so that he could share in our pleasure. Dragging his leg, he would try clumsily to dodge these cascades that flashed in the air like fleeting rainbows. The drops of water scattered over the fire. Utkin's cries of outrage were mingled with the furious hissing of the flames.

Then came the moment of great silence. Our frozen bodies were gradually impregnated with the heat. The smoke enveloped us, tickled our nostrils. We stood stock-still, in the contented torpor of basking lizards. With the transparent dance of the flames. The plenitude of the sun caressing our wet hair. The piercing cold of the river, its rippling, lulling melody. And around us the infinite quiet of the taiga. Its slow breathing, its blue-tinted immensity, dense and profound . . .

It was the throbbing of the engine that shattered our blissful trance. We did not even have time to pick up our clothes. A four-wheel-drive loomed up on the riverbank, turned in a rapid curve, and stopped a few paces from our wood fire.

Samurai and I had barely enough time to cross our hands over our crotches; then we froze, caught off guard in our languid nakedness.

The vehicle had its top down. Apart from the driver, there were two passengers, two young women. One of them in the parked vehicle held out a large plastic bottle to the driver. The man opened his door and set off toward the river.

Dumbfounded, keeping our genitals covered, we stared at the two strangers. The women got up from their seats and perched themselves on the folded top. As if to get a better look at us. Seated on the ground at the other side of the fire, Utkin awaited the outcome of the scene with a mischievous smile, meanwhile stuffing blueberries into his mouth.

The two young women were, no doubt, fledgling geologists; their companion too. Probably students who had come for a period of training on the terrain. Their relaxed air, as of city dwellers, fascinated us.

They stared at us with little sign of embarrassment over our nudity. With the curiosity one has for wild animals at the zoo. They were blond. Our eyes, unaccustomed to differentiating women's faces with precision, took them for twin sisters. . . .

At length one of them, whose stare was more insistent, said to her colleague with a grin: "That little one, he looks like a real angel."

And she gave a slight nudge with her shoulder, glancing at her companion roguishly.

The other one stared at me, but without smiling. I noticed a subtle fluttering of her long eyelashes.

"Yes, an angel, but with little horns," she replied with slight irritation, and without paying us any further attention, she slid down onto her seat.

The driver returned, the full bottle in his hand. The first blond woman, before settling down in her turn, continued to look at me with a persistent smile. And I felt the touch of her look on my lips, on my eyebrows, on my chest, almost physically. . . . At that moment the twin sisters became two totally different women to me. One of them, reserved and sensitive, who seemed as if she had a tense string within her, was a fragile blonde, reminiscent of the splinters of crystal we found in the rocks. The other was amber, warm, enveloping, sensual. So women, too, could be different!

Samurai jerked me out of my reverie by splashing my back with long cold gushes. He was already in the water.

"Utkin," he shouted. "Push him in the drink! I'm going to drown this bare-assed Don Juan!"

"Who's that?" I asked, taking the name for some swear word that was unknown to me.

But Samurai did not reply. He was already swimming toward the opposite bank. . . . We often heard such strange words on his lips. They were doubtless all part of the Olga mystery.

Utkin, instead of pushing me, came up to me and muttered in a dull, broken voice: "Go on, then, swim! What are you waiting for?"

He looked at me. And for the first time I noticed that sorrowful, questioning glint: that effort to fathom the sense of the mosaic of beauty. . . . Then, turning away, he started throwing fresh branches on the fire.

On the way home, I noticed that even Samurai had been affected by the encounter alongside the wood fire. He was trying to find an excuse to talk about the two strangers.

"They must be on the faculty at Novosibirsk," he declared, not finding a better opening gambit.

Novosibirsk, the capital city of Siberia, was almost as unreal to us as the Crimea. Anything that was located to the west of Lake Baikal was already redolent of the Western World.

Samurai was silent. Then, giving me a coarsely flippant look, he remarked: "I'll bet he has those two every day, that driver!"

"Sure, he has them," I said, eager to echo his opinion, as well as his man-of-the-world tone of voice.

The conversational exchange stopped there. We sensed something deeply false in our words. It should have been said differently. But how? Should I speak of the tense string, the crystal, the amber? Samurai would certainly have taken me for a madman. . . .

Utkin only caught up with us close to the ferry. In the taiga, as always, he dragged his foot a hundred yards behind us. But for once we had not heard any of his usual shouts. It was we, in turn, who tried anxiously to make out his figure among the dark tree trunks, as we yelled: "Hey, Utkin! The wolves haven't eaten you up, have they? Ow-ooo!"

The ferry over the Olyei — a great raft of blackened logs — provided a shuttle in summer three times a day. The left bank was us, Svetlaya, the East. The right bank was Nerlug, with its brick houses and the Red October cinema. In short, a more or less civilized city, antechamber to the Western World . . .

The passengers on the ferry were for the most part returning from the city. Their shopping bags were crammed with paper-wrapped packages of provisions that could not be found in the village.

The one-armed ferryman, Verbin, grasped a great paddle with a special groove in it and began to pull on the steel cable, jamming it adroitly. Passing through iron rings on the handrail of the ferry, the cable guided us toward the opposite bank. Samurai took the auxiliary paddle to assist the ferryman.

I sat on the planks that covered the raft. I listened to the soft lapping of the water and absentmindedly watched the village drawing nearer, with its low izbas surrounded by gardens, the maze of paths and fences, the blue smoke rising from a chimney.

The sun was setting above the right bank, on the city side, that of the distant Lake Baikal, that of the Western World. And our village was completely bathed in its coppery light.

When we reached the middle of the river, Utkin nudged me with his elbow, indicating something in the distance with a swift movement of his chin.

I followed his gaze. On the bank where we were to land I saw the figure of a woman. I recognized her easily. She was standing at the water's edge, shading her eyes with her hand and watching the ferry as it slipped slowly across the orange flood of the setting sun.

It was Vera. She lived in a little izba at the edge of the village. Everyone said she was mad. We knew she would stand like that until all the passengers had alighted on the bank and started climbing toward the village. Then she would approach the ferryman and ask him a question in a low voice. Nobody knew either what she said to him or what Verbin replied to her.

For years and years she had been making her way down to the riverbank, waiting for someone who could come only in summer, in the evening, with the dreamlike slowness of this old ferry, blackened by time. She watched, certain that one day she would make out his face in the midst of the crowd in its Sunday best.

When the ferry was close to shore, Samurai abandoned his paddle and came to join us. Like us, he was watching the woman waiting for the ferry to arrive.

"Hey! She must really have loved him!" he said, shaking his head with conviction.

We were the first to jump out onto the sand. And as we passed close to Vera, what we saw in her somber eyes was the death of hope for that day. . . .

The sun, now stranded on top of the taiga on the western bank, might have been the gilded disk of that immobilized pendulum. Time had stood still. The vast swings of days gone by had narrowed down to the back and forth of an old ferry guided by a rusty cable. . . .

When I reached the izba, I took a mirror with an oval frame out of my aunt's chest of drawers and studied myself in it, taking advantage of the pale luminosity of the summer twilight. This study, I knew, was unworthy of a real man. I did not dare to imagine all the taunts of Samurai and Utkin if they had chanced to catch me at this occupation for ladies. But the words of the two blond women were still ringing in my ears: "An angel" . . . "but with little horns." The dull oval, which was slowly growing dim, was crammed with many secrets. So the features it reflected could be loved . . . and make a woman mad . . . and bring her back to the riverbank over long years, with an impossible hope. . . .

A strange confirmation of my first intimations of love came to me on the anniversary of the Revolution.

My aunt had invited three of her best friends, two of whom, like her, worked on the railroad as switch operators; the third worked as a sales clerk in a food store in Kazhdai. They were all single women.

On the table, on a great china dish, there was a block of pork in aspic, looking like a cube of grayish, shiny ice; cold sauerkraut, seasoned with oil and garnished with cranberries; gherkins, of course; stroganina, the fish gelatinized and cut into transparent slices that you eat raw; potatoes with fresh cream; beef rissoles grilled in the stove. And vodka, which they mixed with blueberry syrup.

The sales clerk had brought pancakes, little biscuits, and chocolates, otherwise impossible to find, that she had saved up.

The women drank; as their voices grew soft, it was as if one could hear the chink of the ice breaking, melting. Long live the Revolution! Despite the rivers of blood, it had given birth to this fleeting moment of happiness. . . . Don't think about all the rest! It's too hard; don't think about it anymore! Not this evening, at least . . . It won't bring back their dear faces; or that handful of happy days; or those kisses redolent of the first snows — or was it the last? It's hard to remember now. Or the eyes in which you could see the clouds hurrying toward Lake Baikal, toward the Urals, toward siege-struck Moscow. They set off in pursuit of those clouds, caught up with them at the walls of Moscow, in the frozen fields gutted by the tanks. And they stopped them with their wide-open eyes, staring at them forever as they floated lightly westward. Lying in a frozen rut, their faces buried in the black sky . . .

But let's not speak of it. The first snows, the last snows. . . .

Hold on, Tanya, let me give you this piece; it's not so burned. . . . I had a couple of letters from him, and then . . . Don't think about it. . . . Two letters in two years . . . Let's not think about it. . . .

Perched on the broad, warm surface of the great stone stove, on top of which were piled old felt boots, a woolen blanket, and two limp pillows, I was drowsing. I knew them by heart, these conversations that were forever slipping off into their wartime past. They tried to get away from it and began to talk about the latest village news. Apparently, they said, the headmistress had been seen again with . . . now, what is his name?

It was the singing that came and rescued them from the clouds frozen in the eyes of their fleeting lovers and the gossip several years old. Their voices grew bright, soared. And I was always surprised to see the extent to which these women, these shadowy figures from another era, could suddenly become grave and remote. . . . They sang, and in the haze of my sleep I could picture the horseman battling through a snowstorm and his fair one waiting for him at the dark window. And that other lovesick damsel, begging the wild geese to carry her words to her true love, who has gone "beyond the steppes, beyond the blue sea." And I began to dream of all that might lie hidden beyond this blue sea that had suddenly surged up in our snowbound izba. . . .

My aunt always checked to see if I had gone to sleep before they began to talk about the headmistress's imaginary cavortings. "Mitya!" she would call, turning her head toward the stove. "Are you asleep?" I did not reply. And for good reason. I was absolutely determined not to miss the recital of the latest adventures of the only woman deemed to be capable of having any. I remained silent. I was listening.

This time I heard my aunt's question once again. And then her sigh.

"And there's another worry," she said in a low voice. "As if I didn't have enough on my plate. The girls are soon going to start clinging to him like burrs to a dog's tail. I can see it coming already. . . ."

"That's right," agreed the sales clerk. "With his good looks, Petrovna, you'll have more fiancées than you know what to do with. . . ."

"Oh yes, they'll soon spoil him for you, your Dmitri," put in another friend.

I raised myself on one elbow, listening avidly. Spoil me! I was desperate for a set of instructions for this appalling activity, which I sensed must be intensely voluptuous. But they had already begun to talk about a good recipe for salted mushrooms. . . .

And I was left feeling that even the limp pillow beneath my cheek concealed, within the warmth of its stuffing, a strange disguised concupiscence. The promise of some fabulous night when the hours, the darkness . . . and even the air would have the consistency of flesh and the taste of desire. I saw myself on the banks of the Olyei. Standing stark naked in front of a wood fire. My body pierced through with the icy cold of the water. And one of the blond strangers — crystal or amber: I no longer knew which — was standing on the other side of the flames, naked as well. And she smiled at me, bathed in sunlight, in the rich scent of cedar resin, in the bottomless silence of the taiga. I entered ever more deeply into that moment. I stretched out my hand across the fire to touch that of the stranger. . . . The bank suddenly became white, the silence of the taiga wintry. And the slow eddying of the snowflakes enveloped our bodies in muted sunlight.

4

THAT WINTER SAMURAI and I formed the habit of going to the baths together. . . .

Despite his air of a village tough guy, he was quite a sensitive person. The attitude of the two blond women when we were bathing in the summer had not been lost on him. From that encounter onward he started to treat me as his equal. Even though I had only been fourteen at the time! While he was almost sixteen. A difference that to me seemed infinite.

Utkin never came with us. He washed at baths closer to his izba. He was afraid of freezing his leg.

The baths we went to every Sunday were not different in any way from the others. The little izba was divided into two unequal sections: a small entrance hall, where we left our clothes and our felt boots, then a square room with a bench along one wall and a great stove that heated an enormous cast-iron vessel. We filled it with water from the Brook. All around this bowl was piled up a great heap of pebbles, which quickly became burning hot and had to be sprinkled so that the room should be engulfed in hot steam. Finally there was a kind of little mezzanine, made from two wooden planks, on which you took turns stretching out while your companion whipped you with a bunch of fine birch twigs dipped in the bubbling water. These bunches had been hung up to dry since the summer, under the ceiling in the entrance hall. It was their leaves that, when swollen by the boiling water, made the whole room fragrant with their penetrating scent.

Yes, there was nothing special about the baths. Except that they were located not at the bottom of a kitchen garden but some distance from the village, on the riverbank where the Brook flowed into the Olyei. The izba had been abandoned for years. We had cleaned the great cast-iron bowl and repaired the sunken door. Once established as our Sunday headquarters, the bathhouse seemed to be preparing, through the alchemy of its vapors, for the astonishing transmutation of our bodies. . . .

The cold was such that evening that when we arrived we could no longer feel our numb fingers.

"Forty-eight below!" Samurai exclaimed happily as he slid down the icy path that led toward our baths. "I looked as I went out."

"It'll go down to at least fifty below tonight, that's for sure," I added, understanding his delight very well.

The stars glittered with a shimmering, provocative fragility. The snow spurted up under our feet with a dry, sonorous whispering.

The door was frozen solid. We pushed at it with all our strength. It gave way with a rending squeal, like a smashed windowpane. We lit a candle stuck to the bottom of an empty can. Around its hesitant flame there glowed an iridescent halo. Squatting down, Samurai began to fill the stove: I tore off the birch bark that was needed for the first flames.

Little by little the icy interior of the dark room was coming back to life. Its somber walls, made of logs, became warm. Above the bowl a fine cloud of steam arose.

Samurai filled a ladle and sprinkled the pebbles. The angry hiss was a good sign. We went to undress in the entrance hall, which now seemed arctic. . . .

A true bath should resemble hell. The flames dart through the little door of the stove. As the pebbles are sprinkled more and more copiously, they hiss like a thousand serpents. The planks become slippery. Movements, in the darkness, become clumsy. And as for the bunches of birch twigs, they are a veritable torture! But also an intense pleasure. It is my turn first. I stretch out on the narrow planks of the mezzanine, and Samurai begins to whip me with fury. He dips his bunch of twigs into the boiling water and lashes my back with it. I yell with pain and joy. The fine and supple twigs seem to penetrate between my ribs. My mind is dulled. The steam grows hotter and hotter. With satanic relish, Samurai continues to riddle my back with smarting stabs. Nor does he forget to empty a ladle over the burning pebbles from time to time. For several seconds the fresh cloud of steam hides my torturer. . . .

At length my mind, annihilated by the excess of pain and pleasure, announced to me in its final message that I no longer had a body. It was true! Where my body had once been I experienced a blissful absence, a delicious void made up of misty shadow, of the slightly piquant aroma of birch leaves macerated in boiling water. And also of the rhythmic strokes of the twigs, which were now striking a vacuum, passing through me as if I were air . . .

At that moment, exhausted, Samurai stopped, let fall the bunch of twigs, and stretched out on the planks at right angles to mine. I performed my task while remaining a stranger to my body. It was my arms that rose and fell, flagellating Samurai's muscular back as he groaned with pleasure. Everything happened without my being aware of it. . . .

Strangely enough, it was Samurai's great body that first revealed to me how naked flesh could be beautiful.

The steam was so burning hot that we could no longer breathe. Our heads buzzed, and red bubbles swelled and burst in our eyes. It was time to perform the essential act.

We opened the door to the room, then that to the entrance hall. We rushed outside under the resonant, trembling stars, into the dense cold of the night. . . .

A second later we stopped, naked, at the base of the slope that led down toward the Olyei. One, two, three! and we flung ourselves backward into the virgin snow. We felt no cold. For we no longer had bodies.

The crystalline sound of the stars. The dull sound of our heartbeats. Our hearts seem as if they are abandoned, all alone, sunk in the pure, dry snow. The dark sky draws us into its abyss, crammed with constellations.

An instant . . . And then the wisps of steam that had been rising above us vanished. We began to feel our skin being burned by the melted snow, our shoulders and our wet hair being tugged at by the crust of ice already forming. . . .

We returned to our bodies.

And jumping to our feet with one bound, so as not to spoil the fine imprints we had made in the snow, we ran toward the baths. . . .

That evening Samurai was seated as usual in his favorite tub. It was made of copper that he polished from time to time with sand from the river: almost a little bathtub. He folded up his long legs and immersed himself. I stretched out on a bench.

The room seemed quite different after our mad excursion under the icy sky. The heat was no longer suffocating but swathed our rediscovered bodies pleasantly. The scents were still vivid but more distinct, clarified. It was so delicious to inhale the warm, dry breath of the stones and then, turning one's head slightly, to ingest the scent of a bunch of birch twigs left in the bowl. And to follow the slow progress through the darkness of another odor, that of the bark burning in the stove.

After the frenzy of hell, after the moment of disappearance under the stars, this room, filled with a soft, warm half-light, would become a strange paradise for us as night approached. We would remain still for a long time, dreaming. Then Samurai would light his cigar. . . .

He lit one that evening too. A real Havana, which he drew out of a tube of fine aluminum. I knew cigars like that were sold only in the city, in Nerlug, twenty-three miles from our village, and that they cost sixty kopecks each, including the tube — a fortune! Four school lunches!

But Samurai seemed not to be concerned about the price. He stretched out his arm, seized the ax that was lying near the stove, and, resting his fat cigar on the flat edge of the bathtub, cut off a stray end with a swift and precise action.

After the first puff he settled still more comfortably into the water and announced without preamble, gazing up at the blackened ceiling of the izba: "Olga says that all those little muzhiks who smoke their little cigs, their stinking cigarettes, don't know how to live."

"How do you mean, they don't know how to live?" I asked, lifting my head up from the bench.

"They settle for mediocrity."

"What?"

"Yes, they all want to be average. She's got it right. They all imitate one another. An average job. An average wife. They're average in bed. Mediocrities, you see . . ."

"And you?"

"I smoke cigars."

"It costs more, is that it?"

"Not just that. Smoking a cigar is a — um — a . . . it's an aesthetic act."

"What?"

"How can I explain it? Olga knows how to say it. . . ."

"Aesthet . . . What's that?"

"Well, it's the way. Everything depends on the way you do things and not what you do."

"Well, that's obvious. Or we'd have been flogging each other with nettles. . . ."

"Hm . . . Only you see, Juan, Olga says beauty begins when the way becomes everything. When only the way matters. We weren't flogging each other so as to get clean. Do you understand?"

"No, not really . . ."

Samurai was silent. The aromatic cloud from his cigar drifted above his tub. I sensed that he was trying to find words to express what Olga had explained to him.

"Look," he murmured finally, inhaling a puff, with his eyes half closed. "For example, she says that when you are with a woman, you don't need to have a prick as big as that!" Samurai grabbed the ax and brandished its long, slightly curved handle. "That's not what counts. . . ."

"She talked to you about that?"

"Sure . . . Well, not in those words."

I raised myself on my bench to get a better look at Samurai. I hoped that he was going to reveal a great mystery.

"So. What does count when you 'have' a woman?" I asked in a falsely neutral voice, so as not to disturb his confidences.

Samurai remained silent, then, as if he was disappointed in advance by my incomprehension, he replied a little curtly: "Harmony."

"Huh? Harmony . . . How?"

"Everything being in harmony — lights, smells, colors . . ." He stirred in his tub. Turning toward me, he warmed to his theme: "Olga says a woman's body makes time stand still. By its beauty. Everyone else is running and jumping around . . . and you, you live in that beauty. . . ."

He went on talking, at first hesitantly, then in an increasingly assured voice. He probably had not understood what Olga had confided to him until he began to explain it to me.

I listened absentmindedly. I thought I caught the main drift. What I was seeing again now was the face of the blond stranger on the riverbank. Yes, there was a harmony: the rippling of the Olyei, its coldness, the aromatic breath of the wood fire, the pregnant silence of the taiga. And that feminine presence intensely concentrated in the soft curve of the blond stranger's neck as I stared at her over the dance of the flames.

"Otherwise, Juan, you know, love would be like it is with the animals. Do you remember last summer at the farm?"

Yes, I remembered. It was one of the first warm days of spring. On the way back from school we were crossing the neighboring kolkhoz. Suddenly the furious bellowing of a cow exploded within a long building made of logs, a barn rising up out of thick mud composed of a mixture of snow and dung.

"They must be slaughtering it, the bastards," exclaimed Utkin indignantly, his face distorted with dismay.

Samurai uttered a brief guffaw and beckoned us to follow him. We drew close to the half-open door, lifting our boots with difficulty out of the clinging mud.

Inside, in a section separated from the rest of the barn by a solid barrier of thick planks, we saw a russet cow with fine white patches on its belly. Its legs were shackled. Its head — the horns were cut — was tied to the planks of the barrier. The cow was moving heavily within its enclosure. And an enormous bull was heaving itself up onto the cow's rump with ponderous and ferocious clumsiness. Three men, with the aid of thick ropes, were guiding this relentless assault. The bull had a ring through its nostrils, with a chain attached to it that was being held by one of the men. The bull was uttering ferocious roars as it trampled the muddy ground with its hind feet while with the other two it held the cow's back. That animal's body was supported by a kind of prop, so that its legs should not be broken under this monstrous weight.

The erect thing beneath the bull's belly held our gaze mesmerized on account of the mightiness of its gnarled, purplish shaft. This shaft, glistening with dark blood, was beating heavily against the cow's white rump. A man gave a shout to the one standing closest to the bull. Amid the agitation and trampling, the man addressed seemed not to hear him.

It was at this moment that the bull uttered a deafening groan. We saw the enormous shaft beneath its belly quiver and propel a powerful jet against the white rump. The men began shouting. Then the kolkhoznik who was closest very deftly grasped the shaft and planted it in the right place. The other two men went on yelling and appeared to be bawling him out because he had been slow.

The whole mass of the bull shuddered with ponderous tremors. The props supporting the cow's body shook and gave out repeated creaks. We saw rapid shivers running across the bull's skin. Its bellowing became duller, as if it was out of breath.

The coupling machine slowed down, and as they watched its functioning, the men were already uttering sighs of relief and mopping their sweaty brows.

Outside, in brilliant sunlight, we headed toward Svetlaya. And we felt a painful numbness in all our limbs . . . as one feels after a superhuman effort or a long illness. Utkin looked at the two of us, his face contracted, and exclaimed in a cracked voice: "My uncle's right when he says man is the cruelest animal on earth!"

"Your uncle is a poet." Samurai sighed, smiling. "Like you, Utkin. And poets are always afraid of life. . . ."

"Life?" echoed Utkin in a very sharp tone.

And he walked on faster, pointing his right shoulder toward the sky. His exclamation echoed in my head for a long time. . . .

Samurai was looking at me from his tub. He was clearly waiting for me to reply to a question I had not heard, engrossed as I was in my recollections of that carnal machine at the farm.

"So Olga, who is she?" I asked, to conceal my inattention.

"He who learns much grows old soon," replied Samurai with a vague smile.

He got up slowly, stepping over the edge of the tub. "Let's go; it's late already," he added, throwing my linen towel to me.

On the way back we walked quickly. The bodies we now had beneath our short sheepskin coats were once more susceptible to the cold, as our eyes were to the terrifying beauty of the frozen sky. The sky was no longer drawing us up but bearing down on us with its hard nocturnal clarity. The biting wind lashed our faces.

Olga's izba was at the other end of the village. Before leaving me, Samurai stopped and said in a somewhat strained voice, because his lips were frozen: "She thinks the most important thing is to make a success of your death. That the man who dreams of a fine death will have an extraordinary life. But that's something I don't quite understand yet. . . ."

"Who can make a success of his death?" I asked, parting my lips with difficulty.

Samurai had already turned and taken several paces away from me. He called out into the icy wind: "A warrior!"

5

IT WAS A PHANTOM train, a dream, an extraterrestrial. The peaceful flow of time in the switch operator's house took its rhythm from the thundering passage of it. Every evening.

The little izba, where my aunt spent twenty-four hours at a time on duty, nestled between the taiga, which overhung its roof, and the tracks. It took you a good three hours to get there on foot. But my aunt fixed it with the carriers of wood who passed through the village early in the morning. They gave her a lift as far as the Devil's Bend, where there was a fork in the road. This gave her a good start. She now had only an hour's walk.

The coziness of this shanty had the ephemeral quality about it that you always find in dwellings where you are not really at home.

A narrow iron bed. A table covered with a waxed cloth on which the pattern had long since faded. A cast-iron stove. A few postcards fixed above the bed in the manner of an iconostasis.

The most important object in this small room was a round clock. The front, where the hands were, had come to take on the look of a human physiognomy. On this familiar face we read all the timetables and the delays, linking each hour and each train with a different expression. In this mimicry there was one evocation that I particularly enjoyed on the occasions when I came to spend the evening with my aunt.

This was the moment of dusk. The sun had completed its low course in the winter sky, grazing the dark tips of the pine trees. It was now asleep at the far end of the tracks, in the direction of the city, to the west. I went out and saw the double line of the rails, shining under the hoarfrost and tinted with pink rays. The fog was growing thicker. The mauve light above the snowy tracks was vanishing.

I went into the izba, I heard the gentle hissing of the great kettle on the stove, I saw my aunt preparing supper: a few potatoes, some frozen bacon that she had just removed from a lean-to attached to the izba — our fridge — some tea, and some poppy-seed biscuits. . . . Outside the little window, which was garlanded with arabesques of ice, the blue slowly changed to purple, then to black.

With our last cup of tea we began glancing at the clock face. We already sensed its coming, that train, as it wound its way along, somewhere in the depths of the sleeping taiga.

We went out well in advance. And in the silence of the evening we heard it approaching. First of all a distant murmur that seemed to arise from the depths of the earth. Then the dull sound of a cap of snow falling from the summit of a pine tree. Finally a drumming, more and more resonant, more and more insistent.

When it appeared I had eyes only for the luminous carnival of the coaches. And the locomotive — a real old-fashioned one — with enormous wheels painted red and glittering connecting rods. It looked like a dark monster covered in flakes of hoarfrost. And, on its breastplate, a broad red star! This nocturnal meteor emitted a fierce roar and made us step back several paces with its powerful draft. My aunt flashed her lantern, and I opened my eyes very wide.

The snug comfort that I guessed at behind the brightly lit windows fascinated me. What mysterious beings did that comfort shelter? From time to time I managed to focus on a female silhouette, a couple seated at a little table with two glasses of tea. Occasionally even a shadowy figure reclining on her berth. But such snatched sightings were very rare. Thick hoarfrost or a drawn curtain would make my observation impossible. And yet a glimpsed silhouette was more than enough for me. . . .

I knew that within the train there was one special coach, bearing inscriptions in three languages: Wagon-lit — Schlafwagen — Vagoni-letti. It was in these coaches that the extraterrestrials, which is what people from the Western World were to us, crossed the empire.

I imagined a woman who had been in her compartment for a day already and was going to spend a whole week there! Mentally I pieced together her long journey: Lake Baikal, the Urals, the Volga, Moscow . . . How I longed to be at the side of this unknown traveler! To be within, in the warm and narrow confines of the compartment where you sit so close together that every movement, every look, takes on an erotic significance, especially with the approach of night. And the night itself, with the rhythmic swaying of the car, is long, so long. . . .

But already the snow squall provoked by the passage of this fabulous train was calming down, and all one could see in the cold fog down the track was two red lights fading from view. . . .

I went again to see my aunt in the switch operator's izba one gray afternoon in February. On the path through the taiga I had noticed a strange languor abroad in the air. The blue distance was misty, but this mist did not glitter like the fog of the great frosts. It clouded over the brilliance of the snows, softened outlines. The taiga no longer seemed like a block of ice streaked with the black lines of the pine trees. Not at all. Every tree was alive, awaiting a sign, already recovering from the long immobility of winter.

On the branches of the pine tree that touched the roof of the little house I saw two crows. As they uttered their guttural cries, they seemed to be conversing. And in these cries one could also hear a soft, languorous weariness. Their voices no longer barked out, as in the deep heart of winter, but floated in the pleasantly mild air, occasionally summoning up a lazy echo.

"We're going to have one of those mild spells!" my aunt said to me when I appeared at the door. "And then if it starts to snow it certainly won't stop tonight. . . ."

The misty languor in nature that day was strangely close to me. For several weeks now I had felt within myself — more in my heart than in my head — a bizarre uneasiness. Its presence was so new to me that I experienced it very physically, I could almost touch it, like the box of matches in my pocket. But the reason for it escaped me.

It sometimes seemed to me that it had all begun that evening at the bathhouse when Samurai spoke of the beauty of the female body, which, according to him, made time stand still. From then on, the smell of his cigar gave me the feeling of a singular nostalgia. One of the most terrible kind: for places and faces one has never seen. Which one mourns as being lost forever. Young savage that I was, I could not know that this was simply love that had not yet found its object. This gave it a violent but blind intensity. For instance, just now I had almost started running after the crows as they flew away slowly, hoping to lose myself in the lascivious idleness of their guttural calls. I felt that nature was already instinctively preparing for its amorous rite of spring. I yearned to be a part of it by surrendering entirely. . . . But to whom?

I was angry with Samurai for having talked about all these weighty things — love, life, death — in a way that was incomprehensible to me, rhetorical, bookish. I was used to perceiving life very concretely. Love — and I saw the graceful curve of the beautiful stranger's body beyond the wood fire. Life — and I saw the living procession of faces that gravitated around the three poles of our universe: taiga, gold, camp. Death — a truck sinking slowly beneath the ice in a long hole at that accursed place the Devil's Bend. And also the wolf, large and handsome, that some loggers had killed and then flung down from their tractor near Verbin's izba, calling out to him: "Here! Make yourself a new shapka, grandpa!" The wolf was already rigid, its paws hard, inert. And at the corner of its proud eye there was a great frozen tear. . . .

I wanted to continue experiencing life in only that way, in all its joy and all its sorrow, immediate, unthinking. Samurai, with his unanswered questions, had made me uneasy.

Waiting for the night train seemed to me stupid. Yes, waiting for this famous Transsiberian, with wide eyes and a thumping heart, to catch a glimpse of a shadowy figure who did not even have an inkling of my existence — what stupidity! And how many of these female silhouettes had there been already, whom I had fallen in love with and accompanied on their journey across the empire? Without knowing if beside my beautiful strangers their husbands were snoring peacefully?

I felt disillusioned, duped, almost betrayed by my night-walking woman of the West.

Outside in the gray air swirled the great fluffy snowflakes that everything had predicted. The view above the track was woven with their white filaments.

I went up to my aunt, who was polishing the nuts of the switch system.

"I'm going off," I said, wrapping my hand around the lever.

"What's got into you? Without supper? Just as it's getting dark?"

"No, I've looked — it's only half past six. . . ."

"But by the time you get to the Devil's Bend it'll be night. . . . And besides, take a look at the sky: in an hour we'll have a real blizzard."

She wanted to stop me from going at all costs. Did she even have some kind of presentiment, derived from her acute intuition as a solitary and unhappy woman? She gave me all possible reasons.

"What about the wolves? You know it's not autumn now, when their bellies are full. . . ."

"I've got my pike . . . and something to light a torch with."

Finally she mentioned the temptation that she thought irresistible:

"Don't you even want to wait for the Transsiberian?"

"No, not today," I replied, after a brief hesitation. "Besides, if it really starts to snow there's going to be a hell of a delay to the train."

"Yes, that's true," she agreed, seeing that nothing could stop me.

She slipped several poppy-seed biscuits into my pocket and offered me a box of matches — for all eventualities.

I grasped my pike — a long pole with a steel point. I gave my aunt a farewell wave. And I set off walking beside the track, ahead of the train in one of whose compartments was the unknown woman of my dreams. Who did not yet know that our rendezvous was not going to be kept . . .

The castellated ramparts of the taiga retained their look of happy abandonment and soft idleness. The curtain of snowy plumes enchanted the eye with its silent eddying. The start of a mild, wan evening . . . I had an intense feeling for its beauty and its aroused expectations!

In every movement of the air, woman was present. Nature was a woman! In the intoxicating giddiness of the great flakes as they caressed my face. In the long, languid calls of the jackdaws as they greeted the mild weather. In the heightened tawny color of the pine trunks beneath the damp luster of the melted hoarfrost.

The soft snow, the cries of the birds, the red bark . . . everything was woman. And not knowing how to express my desire for her, I suddenly uttered a terrible animal roar.

And panting heavily, I heard its long echo through the still warmth of the air, into the resounding secret depths of the taiga. . . .

For a while I followed the metal track, walking on the ties. Then, when the rails were covered in ever-deepening snow, I put on my snowshoes and plunged into the forest. To take a shortcut. I decided to go to Kazhdai. I could no longer wait. I needed to know who I was right away. To make something of myself. To give myself a shape. To transform myself, to recast myself. To test myself. And, above all, to discover love. Outflank the beautiful traveler, that glittering woman from the West on the Transsiberian. Yes, before the train passed, I must implant into my heart and into my body that mysterious organ: love.

6

THE TOWN WAS immersed in the dismal daily routine of winter and seemed little inclined to share in my exaltation. Its streets quaked heavily as enormous trucks loaded with the long trunks of cedar trees drove through. Men appeared in the doorway of the only liquor store, thrusting bottles deep into their sheepskin coats. Women, their arms weighed down with shopping bags full of provisions, walked along ponderously, clad in the armor of their thick overcoats. The wind was whipping up and peppering their faces with snow crystals. They had no hands free to wipe them clean. They had to bow their foreheads and from time to time blow noisily, shaking their heads, like horses trying to drive away hornets. Between the men, eager to drown the traces of a hard day in a draft of vodka, and the women, advancing like icebreakers through the raging blizzard, no connection was imaginable. Two alien races. Furthermore, the wind must have caused a power failure. First one side of the street, then the other, was plunged into darkness. The women quickened their pace, gripping the handles of their bags. After a while they all looked so much alike that I thought I was seeing the same faces. As if they had got lost and were walking around and around in that dark town . . .

I, too, spent a good quarter of an hour wandering around under the white flurries, lacking the courage to approach the place where everything was to be acted out: that deserted wing of the station. The place where I could find the one I sought. I already knew what you had to do. I had seen it one day with Samurai. She was sitting at the end of a row of low varnished wooden seats, in that annex to the waiting room where no one was ever waiting for anybody. There was also a buffet, where an attendant, half asleep, shuffled the cups and the sandwiches with slices of shriveled cheese in them. And a newsstand with dusty display shelves, forever closed. And this woman, who from time to time got up and walked over to the timetable board and studied it with exaggerated attention. As if she were searching for some train known only to herself. Then she went and sat down again.

We had seen the man who took a seat beside her, showing her a creased five-ruble bill. We were in front of the newsstand, pretending to be absorbed in the covers of magazines several months old. We had heard their brief whispering. We had seen them go off. Her hair was a dull russet color and covered in an openwork woolen head scarf.

She was the one whom I now saw in the little deserted waiting room. I crossed the resonant space with tense steps, my boots making footmarks on the slippery tiles. She was there, on her seat. My terrified glance only took in the color of her hair. And the outline of her autumn coat, unbuttoned to show a necklace with two rows of red pearls.

I walked up to the closed newsstand. I examined the photo of the latest two cosmonauts, with their radiant smiles, then the smooth face of Brezhnev on another cover. There was no sound other than the creaking of the door in the adjoining main hall and the clink of glasses as the drowsy attendant arranged them in her buffet.

I stared at the shining faces of the cosmonauts without seeing them, but all my senses, like the antennae of an insect, were exploring the tenuous connection that was in the process of being forged between me and the red-haired woman. The dim air of that waiting room seemed to be wholly impregnated with the invisible matter formed by our two presences. The silence of this woman behind my back. Her feigned interest in the muffled loudspeaker announcements. Her real expectation. Her body beneath the chestnut coat. A body in which my desire was already making its habitation. The presence of a woman whom I was going to possess — who did not yet know it. And who was for me a singular and terrifying being in this universe of snow . . .

I detached myself with an effort from the magazine display rack and took several steps in her direction. But involuntarily my trajectory veered away, circled round the seats, and thrust me back in the direction of the main hall. With a thumping heart, I found myself again in front of the timetable board. The Transsiberian was posted there in large letters and several local trains in smaller ones.

I suddenly experienced a faint glimmer of that infinite sadness the red-haired prostitute must have experienced each evening before this board. The cities, the hours. Departures, arrivals. And always this unique Track One. Yes, all the strange trains she apparently missed week after week. She was forever getting up and consulting the timetables so attentively. She strained to hear every word of the croaking loudspeaker. And yet each train would depart without her. . . .

Standing in front of the board, I summoned up all my strength before crossing the threshold of the little room. I checked if my shapka was on my head at a good angle — in an "adult" style, tilted toward one ear, with a few curls showing above my temples. In the cossack manner. In my pocket I fingered the note that had become damp from my burning palm. As unfortunately I had no five-ruble bill but only a three, wrapped around two ruble coins, I told myself there was a risk the Redhead would see this greenish three-ruble bundle and send me packing with a scornful little smile. Neither could I spread out all my treasure before her! And as for trying to change it for a single note, that would have given the game away immediately. Any of the sales assistants would easily have guessed, I thought, what these fateful five rubles were the price of.

In my short sheepskin coat, drawn in at the waist by a soldier's belt of thick leather, with a bronze buckle that bore a well-polished star, I looked like any young logger. This garb, common to all the men in those parts, made my age undetectable. Furthermore, I had a wolf's eyes, gray, tilted back slightly toward the temples. Those of a child born with the eyes of an adult . . .

I took one more look at the departure time of some useless train. I turned. All my anxiety and all the frenzy of my desire were concentrated on the handle of the glass door into the little room. Beyond it was a space filled to overflowing by the rosy glitter of her necklace. . . .

I pulled the handle. This time I went straight toward the red-haired woman without turning aside. . . . I was two steps from her when the light went out. There were several squawks of alarm from passengers in the main hall, several curses, the footfalls of a railroad worker sweeping the darkness with his lamp.

We found ourselves on the platform, she and I, under the white tide of the storm. It was the only place that was more or less lit. By the lights of the Transsiberian, ponderously strung out now, as it flowed into the station. Panting and all covered in snow, the locomotive threw a long beam of light through the white blizzard from its front spotlight. The windows of the coaches cast rectangles of soft light onto the platform. The snowy eddies hurtled toward these yellow rectangles, like moths toward the halo of a streetlamp.

Soon the few passengers due to board the train at this station had climbed into their coaches. Those due to get off had already plunged out into the storm, into the winding streets of Kazhdai. . . . We were left alone, she and I. Travelers without luggage, poised to leap onto the footboard when we heard the whistle? Or improbable relatives determined to wait until the end . . . until the very last glimpse of the face of a dear one as it was carried away into the night?

At our backs we sensed the gaze of Sorokin, the formidable militiaman, who was pacing up and down on the snow-covered platform, with his nose buried in the broad collar of his sheepskin coat. He, too, was waiting for the departure whistle. He seemed to be hesitating: Should he go and corner the Redhead and extort three rubles from her, his usual tax? Or nab the young peasant, me, drag him off into a little smoke-filled office and have some fun scaring him for part of the night? What disconcerted this obtuse, dull man was us as a couple. Conscious of the menacing presence of this dubious guardian of the peace, we had gradually drawn closer to each other. Together, we were becoming strangely unassailable. In particular, I was protecting her. Yes, I was protecting this tall woman clad in an autumn coat that scarcely covered her knees. With my hand on my belt buckle, I stuck out my chest and fixed my eyes on the lighted square from the window that she, too, was staring at. The militiaman could not quite dissociate the two of us: what if this young village boy were some nephew or cousin of the Redhead?

The fresh snow held the imprint of our footsteps, which had drawn imperceptibly closer to one another. And behind the window, in a snug compartment, the silhouette of a woman could be made out. The calm gestures of the evening; the great glass of hot tea that you have to blow on for a long time; the absent gaze into the white storm rattling against the window. The gaze settles distractedly on two shadowy figures in the middle of the empty platform. What on earth could they be waiting for there?

Aroused by the whistle, the train moved off and withdrew the illuminated square from under our feet. The station was still in complete darkness. We could exist as a couple for only a few more seconds. . . .

It was by the light of the last coach that I abruptly produced my five rubles. She saw my gesture, smiled a little disdainfully (no doubt she had guessed the point of my comings and goings in the waiting room), and inclined her head slightly. I did not know whether this was a refusal or an invitation. I followed her anyway.

We walked for a long time along narrow alleys, beside fences covered in snow. The blizzard had by now spread its wings with unbridled force, hurling volleys of snow against our faces and taking our breath away. I walked behind the red-haired woman, who was holding the woolen head scarf knotted under her chin with one hand and, with the other, beating down the panels of her coat. Every so often I saw her legs uncovered, and then my mind went blank, stunned as I was by the whistling of the wind and drained by the sharpness of my desire.

"Where are we going?" said a strange, heavy voice inside me. "And what hidden meaning do these powerful legs have, with their broad thighs and their full calves squeezed into black leather boots? And this body with its flimsy coat? What connects it to me?" This body beneath its thin covering of fabric. Its warmth, which I felt had already profoundly entered into me . . . "Why this warm and vital density, under this cold sky, amid these dead streets?"

We tramped for a long time through the dark, white town. Advancing through a storm, confronting the snow flurries, makes you weary. The crunch of footsteps; the whispering of the wind sliding in under the fur of your shapka and murmuring into your ear the lament of the snowflakes melting on your face . . . At one moment I smelled the scent of burning cedarwood, of a fire, floating in the wind. I raised my head. I looked at the woman walking in front of me. I saw her quite differently. It suddenly seemed as if she were taking me to a house that had been waiting for me for a long time, that was my real home; and as if this woman was the being closest to me. A being I had miraculously rediscovered in this snowstorm.

It was an izba at the very edge of the town, a building tucked away at the bottom of a little snow-covered yard. The red-haired woman — who had not spoken a word to me since the station — all of a sudden smiled and exclaimed almost cheerfully, as she mounted the wooden steps: "Here we are. Welcome to the mariner!"

Her voice had a strange resonance at this frontier between the white fury of the storm and the dark interior of the izba. A phrase from some ritual she made a point of performing once the frontier was crossed. Here was where I became her man, her client.

We passed through the shadowy entrance hall and climbed several stairs, which groaned under our feet. She pushed open the door, patted the wall, trying to find the switch, and pressed it several times. Then uttered a forced giggle: "Oh, silly me! The whole town's playing blindman's buff, and there's me saying: Come on, dynamo — get turning!"

I heard her opening a drawer and striking a match. The room was lit up by the diffuse halo of a candle. No doubt it was this flickering flame that fragmented my perception. Gestures, words, and smells began to materialize out of the wavering darkness. One by one, randomly. And they cast their own shadows — of gestures, words, and smells.

Her profile appeared sharply on the wall — black on yellow. So did the glass whose brown contents she poured between her lips, lapping them up avidly. She filled the same glass, held it out to me. I recognized the local brew: alcohol mixed with cranberry jam. It flooded into me, like one of the shadows flitting across the bare wall of the izba. It burned, flayed my palate, filled me with darkness. As before, I could see only fragments. But the candle had remained in the room next door, and these shards were fading, becoming dull. Everything was splitting up. One piece: her torso rearing up before my eyes, strongly, terrifyingly white. (One could never have imagined how broad it would be!) The whiteness tinged with yellow shadow. This bright patch was suddenly drowned in the darkness that erupted, causing an explosion of metallic creaks from the bed. Another fragment: her hand, large and red, pulling the blanket over my bare shoulder. With an absurd solicitude and insistence. And then a china statuette on the shelves by the bed: a slender ballerina with her partner. I saw their smooth faces, their unmoving eyes, very close to me.

And all that happened in the hollow of this bed, with its smell of cold smoke and sugary perfume, was only a series of abrupt, hopeless attempts to join the odd fragments together.

By accident and in my fear of not doing what a man had to do, I caught hold of a breast, heavy and cold. It did not respond to the clasp of my fingers. I let it go, as one lays a dead bird down in the grass. I tried with all my weight to crush the body that spilled off into the shadows, to keep it together in the unity of my desire. I buried my face in the russet curls. And once more I came up against a separate shard — the drops of melted snow in her hair. And an earring, quite simple and worn, sliding toward my lips . . .

I had expected love to have the intensity of my nocturnal plunge into the snow with Samurai, beneath the frozen sky: that unique moment when the heat of the bath and the cold of the stars produced a searing fusion. I had expected that there would be nothing to touch, to feel, to recognize, for everything would be a single incandescent touching. And that I would be wholly outside and inside, the organ of that indescribable touching . . .

The red-haired prostitute must have sensed that I was at a loss. She parted her legs heavily to let me slide into her groin. Her body gathered itself up, became taut. Her hand penetrated under my belly, grasped me, thrust me into her. With a precise, deft movement. She seemed to be putting me in tune with her body, plugging me into her flesh. . . . And rearing up slightly, she shook me, pushed me into action.

I writhed between her broad thighs. I clung onto her breasts, which yielded with a soft, lazy resignation. My belly seemed to be stretching a great hot, sticky wound beneath her.

So this was the stuff of love: slippery, glutinous. And lovers were heavy, breathless. It was as if each, laboriously, were hauling the other one's body along. . . . But where to?

All that I understood only later. I lived through it again when, bowed under the snow squalls, I was running to get away from the bed with its slimy depths, and the izba that smelled of cold smoke. My cheek was burning from two terrible blows. The red-haired prostitute had slapped me with a hoarse exclamation and a look filled with hate.

I was running toward the great bridge that spanned the Olyei. I was plunging into the white tide without thinking about what I was going to do. Everything was too clear for it to be thought about. As clear as the white abyss that opened at my feet on the crown of the bridge. It was in this abyss that I must flee the stare of the red-haired woman. Her look and the horrible mess that was love. Climb over the handrail and escape from the vision that was gradually becoming more vivid in my head . . .

This vision had arisen when, in the midst of my feverish thrashings on her great body, the light shone. Absurdly, the electricity had come on again. The room was frozen by the ghastly, stunning light of a great bulb. The red-haired prostitute screwed up her eyes, her face twisted into a grimace of disgust. I stared at this broad face.

This heavily made-up mask. This tired paint. These shining pores. I sensed that the harsh light made it vulnerable, trapped by the stupid return of the current. But I, too, was caught in the trap. I could not turn my gaze elsewhere. The mask held it. I was thrashing around, my face a couple of inches away from that unhappy grimace. I felt a strange pity for the mask, and it was at that moment that my desire exploded.

I did not know, then, if what I experienced was fear, pity, love, or disgust. There was that face, with its pathetic grimace; the red lips with a sickening breath of alcohol; the dark-red hair spangled with drops of water. . . . And this violent spasm wrenching my stomach — in a warped replica of our nocturnal ecstasy in the snow on the banks of the Olyei.

I caught just a glimpse of the glittering night sky, filled with constellations. . . . Then the red-haired prostitute let her thighs fall back and pushed me away slightly, to free herself. She was unplugging me from her body. . . .

There was none of the humid warmth of the bath for me to get into. None of the intoxicating smell of Samurai's cigar. A pitiless light with a dry and powdery whiteness. I saw the red-haired woman get up and stand in the middle of the room. Her nakedness terrified me. Especially viewed from behind. I hoped she was going to put out the light. But she started to dress. Her body went through the actions with difficulty, balancing clumsily now on one leg, now on the other. From time to time I saw her profile bending over the garments she was buttoning up. Her lips moved slowly, as if she were addressing silent words to herself. Her eyelids were heavy with sleep. The alcohol must be affecting her more and more.

Finally she turned around, probably to urge me to hurry. Her gaze met mine. Her eyes grew wide. She saw me! Her lips trembled. Putting her great hand to her mouth, she repressed a cry. Only a kind of dull choking sound was heard.

Leaving her blouse half unbuttoned, she rushed to a little

cupboard, opened it with a violent movement, and took out a bottle. Then, without offering me the slightest explanation, she sat on the edge of the bed beside me and flung back the blanket. I had no time to react. She poured what I took to be water into the hollow of her palm and began to rub my genitals and the lower part of my belly vigorously. Dumbfounded, I allowed this to be done to me. The rubbing burned my skin: the water turned out to be alcohol. . . . Every now and then the woman gave me a look that I could not understand. It was both sorrowful and pitying. Like the one I would observe in Utkin's mother when she saw her son limping across the courtyard.

Besides, there was no longer anything to understand. What I was experiencing simply could not be thought about at all. The burning of the alcohol, equally incomprehensible, was welcome, rather: it corresponded to the intoxication that was slowly invading every corner of my being.

It was this drunkenness that freed me from all amazement. What was happening to me was becoming absurdly natural: both the red-haired woman, who, before putting away the bottle, filled herself a glass right to its lipstick-stained brim; and the light that suddenly went out again; and the packet of old photos she fetched at the same time as the candle. . . .

Everything was natural. This great woman in her unbuttoned blouse sitting beside me, laying out these black-and-white snapshots on the blanket. She wept silently, whispering explanations that I could not hear. I did not see the photos; I lived their tarnished images. There was almost always a young, smiling woman, shading her eyes from the sun. In her arms she held an infant who looked like her. Sometimes a man appeared beside them, dressed in wide trousers and an open-necked shirt such as nobody had worn for a long time now. And I breathed the air of these unknown days that I recognized by the flickering light of the candle. A fragment of river, the shadow of a forest. Their looks, their smiles. Their family complicity. In spite of myself, I experienced the happiness of these unknown people.

The commentaries the red-haired woman gave me through her silent tears constantly referred to that heavenly summer. And then came the fateful dissolution of the warmth focused on these yellowed snapshots. Someone had gone away, disappeared, died. And the sun that had made the young woman screw up her eyes in those photos had given way to the deceptive halo of the night trains at the snow-covered station in Kazhdai. . . .

The edges of the photos had been carefully shaped. The person who had trimmed them must have dreamed of the long family history they would one day evoke, gathered together in an album. I picked up a photo and stroked the trimmed edge: I felt the breeze of the sunny days on my face, I heard the laughter of the young woman, the crying of the baby. . . .

The candle flame was flagging, flickering; the storm rattled noisily in the chimney; the fire, revived, embalmed the darkness with warm, penetrating odors. My drunkenness detached this moment from what had gone before. The red-haired woman's izba became my rediscovered home. And this woman sitting beside me was someone close to me, whose absence, from now on, I would be aware of.

When there were no more photos, the woman tried to smile at me through the mist of her tears. Closing her eyes, she leaned toward me. With a tentative hand, I touched her shoulder. Everything was mixed up in my wine-soaked young head. The woman was this body and this stormy night and this moment with the smell of the fire . . . and this rediscovered being. I wanted to cling to her, to live in the shade of her body, by the rhythm of her silent sighs. Not to depart from this moment.

She touched my forehead with her chin. My hands brushed

against the collar of her blouse, touched her breasts. I closed my eyes. . . .

She pushed me away violently. On the wall I saw the rapid swing of a shadow. My head was shaken by two resounding slaps. I came to my senses.

She was standing up, her face closed, hard.

"I . . . What . . . ?" I stammered, completely lost.

"Beat it, quick, you dirty little shit!" she said in a weary, disgusted voice.

And in one armful she threw my clothes at me.

If I did not hurl myself into the white abyss right away, it is because when I reached the crown of the bridge I became aware that there was no longer any me. There was no longer a person to be hurled into the icy river.

There was certainly a ghost from before — that adolescent who would avidly seize on any tale of love; that spy on sexual confidences let fall by the hulking great loggers in the workers' canteen. An unrecognizable ghost.

And there was that other one who, a few moments before, was thrashing around between the thighs of an unknown woman, his eyes fixed on her face with the pitiless light beating down on it. That one, too, was a stranger.

As for the one who had just been exploring old photos, this was a being I had never encountered within me. . . .

I found myself on the bridge with several scraps of myself being scattered into the snow-lashed darkness. The wind was so violent that it seemed to empty my body of all the warmth from my short sheepskin coat. I could no longer feel my lips, or my cheeks, now covered with a layer of crystals. I no longer existed.

Unhappiness and madness have their own logic too. . . .

It was in accordance with this logic that the bridge suddenly lit up. The headlights of a truck, late, untimely, fortuitous, crazy. The driver should have crossed the bridge at full speed and disappeared in pursuit of his own obscure goal. But he braked abruptly. For — that was it — he had no goal. Other than this absurd race through the storm. Quite simply he was drunk. Drunk and sad. Like the brawl he had just been involved in on the steps of the liquor store under a dim streetlamp. The light had gone out, and he could not even hit the man who had cut his cheek with a fragment of bottle glass. Cursing, they had gone their ways into the darkness. . . .

Now it was vital not to stop. The two patches of yellow from the headlights were the only source of light, the throbbing of the engine was the only reservoir of warmth. Yes, his drunken heartbeats and that engine. Despite the snow, the whole universe was black.

And if he stopped suddenly on the crown of the bridge, it was because he must have detected the presence of a tiny parcel of life in this icy pass. He saw a shadowy figure transfixed behind the parapet, clinging to the cast-iron railing. A shadowy figure that seemed to be waiting for the ultimate extinction of its last spark. When the numbed fingers let go . . .

Or maybe, quite simply, he saw this solitary silhouette and his cloudy brain imagined a woman. One he could accost and cheer up with whatever was left of the vodka in the bottle he kept hidden behind the seat. Some desperate girl whose whole life had been rather like this teetering on the parapet of a bridge at night. A crumpled body he could lay down on the narrow bench behind the seats. A woman he could "have."

Or maybe he guessed what kind of shadowy figure it was; and felt bad about his own thoughts; and would even have had pity on that frozen girl he wanted to drag into his cabin.

Maybe . . . Who knows what went on inside the head of a drunken Siberian truckdriver, a big, rough man, his forearms covered by tattoos (anchors, crosses on a tombstone, women with big breasts), with one cheek covered in dried blood, and sad gray eyes that were forced to peer out through a fog of drunkenness?

He saw a shadowy figure, thought of an easy body stretched out on the bench, felt a pleasant heaviness at the base of his stomach. And he was angry; the whole of life is governed by this heaviness. Food, woman, blood!

He braked and jumped down into the snow, slamming the door. Rubbing his cheek with a ball of ice scooped up from the slatted side of the truck, he walked toward the shadowy figure. You could no longer see anything three yards ahead. The waves of snow were so dense that you would have thought the earth itself was rocking and tipping into the Olyei.

The figure stood behind the parapet, above the white abyss of the river. The driver tapped it on the shoulder. Then he cast a look down below. His eyes opened wide. It was the void: the invisible frontier of a vertiginous beyond. He grabbed the collar of the snow-covered sheepskin coat and pulled the figure over the parapet.

"What the hell are you doing there?" he demanded, dragging his burden toward the truck. "Where'd you get pissed like that, idiot? Why, at your age I was sweating my guts out in the factory! And today all these kids can think about is getting pissed out of their skulls."

The shadowy figure made no reply. In any case the truckdriver was really asking himself these questions, while thinking about something quite different. About that nameless abyss, about the solitude he had just encountered in the night, about the fine trickle of warmth the frozen ghost was still giving off.

He went on talking in the same way in the cabin. The storm wind had woken him up, had made him garrulous. These snatches of nighttime conversation were the first things I was aware of when, slowly, I began to reinhabit the inanimate ghost shaken by the jolting of the road.

I was warming up, becoming myself again. I needed to assume my new identity. The unrecognizable strangers were once again assembling within me: the virgin of a few days ago who spied on adult confidences; the young frenzied body ripping the belly of a prostitute with his sex; and the figure in the storm, waiting to take the final step, waiting for his numbed fingers to give way. . . . All this was me!

The man asked where I lived and read my reply in the quivering of my lips, which I could still hardly control. I stared at him. His face swollen from the cold, the alcohol, and the blows he had just received. His broad, hairy wrists. His hands covered in shiny scars, his thick fingers with their broad, hardened nails . . .

And without being able to reach the logical conclusion of my thought, I was feeling: Now I am like him; yes, I am in the same boat he is; in his skin, pretty much. Instead of the immense joy that, for years, I expected at this turning point of my life, a cruel despair! Like him . . . Soon the same tattooed hands on the steering wheel of a heavy truck, the same face, the same smell of vodka. But above all the same experience with women. I gave a sidelong glance at his heavy legs and imagined the force with which they would part a woman's thighs. The thighs of a woman . . . Of the red-haired woman! I felt something tremble inside me: of course he had "had" her. Before me . . .

"So what are you gawking at me like that for?" he muttered, noticing how intently I was staring at him. "One thing's for sure: we can't go any faster. Have you seen the road?"

At each stroke the windshield wipers flung aside a thick layer of clinging snow. It seemed as if only the taiga was guiding the truck, as it plowed on into the storm.

I looked away. No further need to look at my man: he was an exact replica of me in a few years' time. . . .

Now I knew precisely what was going to happen. I knew that we had only a few minutes left to live!

I was waiting for the Devil's Bend. Drunk as he was, the driver was sure to miss it. I could already picture the long sideways slide of the truck, the frantic and useless wrenching of the steering wheel; I heard the engine choking in an impotent roar. I saw the black breach in the ice, which was always very thin at that point on account of warm springs in the bed of the Olyei.

I swallowed my saliva nervously, focusing on the road. I was like the bullet in a revolver primed for firing. Abrupt burning thoughts, searing images, propelled the tension to its peak. Those hands resting on the steering wheel had crushed the breasts of the red-haired woman. We had both of us been ensnared in the same moist wound at the base of her belly. We would both of us be forever floundering in the same narrow space at the edge of the endlessness of Siberia: the dreary streets of the district center; the cabins of trucks stinking of diesel oil; the taiga — wounded, pillaged, hostile. And that red-haired woman. Open to all. And this stormy night that cut us off from the world. And this tiny cabin crammed with homogeneous soiled flesh that was going to disappear. As my fingers gripped the door handle, the nails became white. . . .

The driver braked and shouted at me, grinning: "Before that bitch of a corner I need to take a leak. . . ."

I saw him open the door, climb onto the running board, and begin to unbutton his padded pants. My anticipation had been so frenzied that I perceived in his smile a hidden meaning, which seemed to be saying: Ha ha! So that's it, you little squirt — you thought you had me with your goddamned bend. Well, I'm not stupid.

I understood that this dark and absurd world was also endowed with wily and sly cunning. It wasn't so easy to annihilate it by killing yourself. Even as it slid along the razor's edge, this world knew how to stop abruptly and smile with cunning geniality. "A red-haired woman, you say? Some photos spread out on a blanket? First love?

Solitude? Well, look at me! I'm going to unbutton my pants and piss on every one of your first loves and solitudes!"

I jumped down from the truck and began to run in the opposite direction, following the tracks of its wheels. . . .

Against all expectation, I heard neither shouts from the man nor the noise of the engine. No, the driver did not call out, did not rush off in pursuit of me, did not make a U-turn to catch up with me. . . . When I stopped after twenty yards I could no longer see the outline of the truck, could hear no noise. The white blizzard, the fierce whistling of the wind in the branches of the cedar trees, nothing more. The truck had vanished! As I continued on my way, I wondered whether the red-haired woman, the bridge, and that drunken driver had not been a dream. A kind of delirium similar to the one I had once had when ill with scarlet fever . . . Even the wheel tracks I was following were becoming less and less visible and soon disappeared. . . .

I found the dark streets of Kazhdai again. Instinctively, I headed for the station. I went into the barely lit main hall. In fact, it was largely the white reflection of the blizzard that filled this deserted space with a somewhat ghostly luminosity.

I went up to the clock. It was half past ten. The Transsiberian had left at nine. Dumbfounded, I could not manage to do the simple arithmetic, so astounding did the answer seem to me. All that had been lived through in no more than an hour and a half! The interminable wait in front of the newsstand; the Redhead's izba; her body and that pain they called "love"; my flight; the frozen eternity on the bridge; the drunken truck . . . Its disappearance. My return.

Then, as if to add to the unreality of what I was living through, I heard a voice behind my back, probably that of the deputy station-master, explaining to some passenger: "Oh, you know. It'll be when it stops snowing. . . . As you saw, even the Transsiberian had to come back. It'd hardly left the station and there was already three feet of snow on the track. . . ."

I pushed open the glass door and went out onto the platform. So this mass of sleeping coaches was the Transsiberian. Its windows gleamed feebly with the blue reflection of the night-lights on the compartment ceilings. Behind the tracery of hoarfrost you could sense the silent comfort within. And the presence of the beautiful Western woman, who had kept our rendezvous after all. I remembered her, or, more precisely, how I used to spy on her in the old days near the switch operator's izba. My memories of all that were so intense that the events of this evening were now firmly transformed into no more than a particularly vivid daydream. Afraid of shattering this certainty, I went back into the station. So nothing at all had happened. Nothing . . . Nothing!

The door opposite, the one that led out onto the square in front of the station, opened. In the dim light of the main hall I saw a woman coming in, glancing rapidly around her. She was wearing an autumn coat and a thick woolen shawl. She came up to me, as if finding me there were the most natural thing in the world. I watched her approaching. It seemed to me that she no longer had a face. Her features, without makeup, washed out — cleansed by the snow or by tears — were only pale watercolor outlines. All one saw of her face was the expression: an intensity of extreme suffering and weariness.

"Come on. You're going to spend the night at our house," she said in a very calm voice that could only be obeyed.

≈ 7 ≈

IN MY DREAM the corridor of the sleeping car led to a compartment that was a replica of the switch operator's izba, but still smaller. As if that house, being a part of the corridor, were perched on the track, waiting for an improbable departure. A woman was seated at the little table under the window of this strange — but quite natural — compartment. She seemed to be staring out into the darkness of the night outside the window. Not in order to see what the thick hoarfrost was hiding, but so as to avoid seeing what was happening around her. At the center of the little table there was an extraordinary fleshy bulb, cut in two. Inside it could be seen a kind of cocoon composed of semitransparent leaves, delicately folded over one another. It resembled a carefully swaddled baby.

I was supposed — I did not know why — to unwrap its fragile leaves without attracting the attention of the silent passenger. My numb, clumsy fingers were fumbling with this cocoon, this silken cone. I already sensed that what would appear would be painful to see. . . . The further I progressed with my meticulous efforts, the more my anxiety about this revelation increased. I was going to see a living thing whose birth would be compromised by my curiosity but whose vitality I could ascertain only by stripping off the leaves. I was killing it by opening the bulb. But it would not have existed if I had not dared to rip open the cocoon. In my dream the tragic significance of my action did not appear so clearly. It was the slow upsurge of a harrowing cry that expressed it. A cry that rose to my throat — a dry, strangled cry. My fingers were stripping off the leaves with scant ceremony. And the woman sitting by the window began, at that moment, to turn her head slowly in my direction. . . . The cry burst forth, shook me, woke me up. . . .

I saw the halo of a candle and the face of the red-haired woman — an oval, calm, subdued. Her hand was lightly stroking my head.

Seeing me awake, she smiled at me and blew out the candle. I quickly screwed up my eyes. I wanted to go to sleep again before she took away her hand. . . .

After tea in the morning she said to me in a neutral voice, as if it were a trivial daily occurrence: "We've got snow up to the chimney. It's midday already, but look at the windows: it's pitch dark."

"I'll make a passage!" I exclaimed joyfully. "I know how to do it! You'll see. . . ."

"No, no! You just dig a hole for yourself and then go. . . ."

I did not argue. I understood that my joy was stupid. I must go. Quickly. Without looking back . . .

With my snowshoes attached to my belt, I hurled myself at the wall of snow that rose outside the front door. I became mole, snake, and dolphin all at the same time. I dug, wriggled, swam. I battled away at the heart of a white landslide, climbing up within its tide, which grew darker the farther I moved from the house. The rush of snow even penetrated my body, burned it, making my progress more fraught. I opened my mouth to inhale rare puffs of air and swallowed spurts of crystals that stung. My eyelids were immobilized, weighed down with minuscule ice diamonds. At one stage I felt as if I no longer knew the right direction and had lost my sense of up and down. I was surely crawling horizontally, within this mass where there was less and less air left. Or, worse, I was thrusting down into its depths. Such moments of panic are almost inevitable for someone clearing a way for himself after a great snowstorm. My heart thumped. Convulsively, I realigned the angle of my scaling upward. I mounted toward the light like a fish thrusting upstream against the current in a waterfall. . . .

With a resounding crack, my head broke the fine layer of ice.

Dazzled, I stretched out on the smooth, sparkling surface. The sunny air resounded with freshness, seemed as if it were quite a different substance from what I had been breathing hitherto. The sky, revitalized by the mild spell, extended as far as the eye could see. The silence of the taiga was so deep that all the little sounds gathered around me, coming only from my movements — the crunch of snow under my elbow; the echo of my hungry breathing; the resonant slithering of white slabs breaking as they fell from my shapka, from the collar of my sheepskin. . . .

All I could see of Kazhdai was a few dark patches: the roofs of the tallest houses. Some straight outlines as well: the buried trains sleeping on the tracks. I could identify streets thanks to the columns of white smoke rising from the chimneys. The tiny black dots were the inhabitants busy around these columns, making passageways.

The house I had just left was a little distance from the town, at the edge of the taiga. Its smoke seemed as if it were rising from the midst of a deserted plain. And on the branch of a birch tree, buried in the snow, I saw a miniature house designed to give shelter to the birds.

I put on my snowshoes and went up to the solitary chimney. Bending toward its mouth, which was shielded by a pitch-black iron cap, I uttered a resounding yell. It was the custom. The signal for the person left behind . . . I heard the creaking of the stove door, then an echo that seemed to come from the depths of the earth. A kind of slow sigh that was dissipated in the dazzling clarity of this day after the storm . . .

I glided briskly along on my snowshoes, crossing the valley that ran down to the Olyei. The taiga, half awake, stayed beside me at a distance. Great pine trees covered in snow had within their shade the brilliance of a bluish, transparent silver. And their tops glittered, dusted with nuggets of gold.

From time to time I glanced behind me. The column of smoke in the midst of the plain still marked the entombed izba, that room buried beneath the snow, the flickering light of a candle, that interior where the darkness of a winter's night still reigned. An unreal evening spent beneath the compact silence of the snows . . . The red-haired woman!

I remained still for a moment. I gazed at the plain with its thousands of crystals, flooded with sunlight, the endless sky extending its blue freshness; the mother-of-pearl shadow of the taiga. And in the distance, that column of smoke, white, all alone, in the midst of it all . . . Suddenly, with an unbearable clarity, I understood: I am condemned both to this beauty and to the suffering that it conceals. The snow would melt. Kazhdai would become a dark little town once again. The Transsiberian would move off and make up for its delay. And the red-haired prostitute would return to the waiting room. There could not be any other life.

For some time I followed the ample curve of the Olyei, overhung with immense dunes of snow.

Passing close to the three legendary cedar trees, where they hanged the men in the civil war, I stopped, stupefied. This morning the great rusty nails, which I was used to seeing high above me as I tilted my head back, were within easy reach. Yes, they were there, immediately before my eyes. I went up to them and, taking off my mittens, touched the rough brown metal. A slow cold, accumulated over long decades, invaded my fingers. I quickly withdrew my hand. I caressed the rough scales of the trunk. They seemed to harbor a warmth that was sleeping but alive. And suddenly what had happened long ago at the foot of these giant trees — that brutal but swift death — did not seem to me all that terrible. A moment of sharp pain and then this silence in the sun-drenched air, this secret life, sleeping, in perfect fusion with the breathing of this great trunk, with the sharp smell of the clusters of needles, with the glittering of the resin frozen in the indentations on the bark. This life without thoughts, without memories. This oblivion.

I gripped the great nail, I leaned my full weight on it. With half-closed eyes, I tried to enter into that narrow zone which separated me from the blissful silence of the trunk. . . .

Suddenly, through my closed eyelids, I saw them: two black specks were following the blue ridge of the snowdrifts above the riverbank. Soon they were on a level with the three cedars. They hurtled down the ridge and crossed the Olyei. Their tiny silhouettes were becoming more and more distinct. The first of them moved forward with long strides, stopping at intervals to wait for the other one. I recognized them. And I was struck by their rustic and naive appearance. There was something childish about their sheepskins and their faces, which I could see more and more clearly. The earflaps of their shapkas bounced up and down — dogs' ears. They turned the corner by the forest, and in a few moments they were going to pass beside me. I wanted to run away. To hide deep among the snowy pine trees. I was certain I could no longer be a part of their lives. . . .

But already the first of the skiers, Samurai, had noticed me. His harsh cry broke the silence. He came toward me.

Smiles, greetings, teasing. They gave me friendly pats on the shoulder. Told me the latest news from the village. . . .

"They are children," observed some voice deep within me. "Absolute children, carefree and divinely insubstantial."

It seemed inconceivable that only yesterday morning we had been at school together. That only yesterday I had been like them.

"Have you swallowed your tongue or what?" exclaimed Samurai, shoving my shapka down onto my eyebrows. "Look at him, Utkin. He's not a Don Juan anymore. He's a bear that's half asleep!"

Tears came to my eyes. I was so jealous I could have howled. To be like them once again. To glide across the plain, light as the wind, as translucent as this sun-drenched air, as fresh as the breath of the taiga. Innocent!

Samurai must have noticed my tortured expression. He turned away and called out as he sped off, without looking at me: "Come on! There's no time to lose. Otherwise there won't be any seats left. Get going, you sleeping bear! You sleeping beauty!"

I followed them automatically, without even asking where we were going.

After we had been on the move for an hour I saw that Samurai, following an oblique course, was moving away from Kazhdai and heading toward a distant gray cloud that hung above the taiga — toward the city, toward Nerlug.

Another two and a half hours to go, I thought bitterly. Why am I trailing after them? What business do I have in that city?

Now they were walking side by side, chatting. Everything was so luminous, so serene, in the sunny little world that traveled with them. My gaze reached it as if from the depths of a prison cell. From time to time Samurai turned and called out to me cheerfully: "Come on, bear, move your great paws!"

It was no longer jealousy I felt toward them but a sort of malevolent contempt. Especially toward Samurai. I remembered his long discourses at the baths. About women. About love. His endless quotations from that old madwoman Olga. What was it he had said? "Love is harmony." What an idiot! Love, my dear Samurai, is an izba that smells of cold smoke. And the horrible solitude of two naked bodies under a garish yellow lightbulb. And the ice-cold knees of the red-haired prostitute that I brushed against when it was over, when I slid out from her belly, which had shaken me around in the damp hollow of the bed. And the bleary features of her face. And her heavy breasts, stretched by so many callused, blind, hasty hands. Like the hands of my phantom truckdriver — covered with scars, stained with grease. Oh, Samurai, if you had seen him! Before tackling the Devil's Corner he unbuttoned his pants and with his hand took out this huge swollen flesh; it looked like a huge piece of raw, warm, flaccid meat. Don't talk to me about love. . . . And you will be like him, Samurai, in spite of your cigar and all that rubbish Olga tells you. You won't get away from it! Nor will I, or even Utkin. And we shall stay in this district center where the endless brawling stops only when the light goes out in a snowstorm. In our village, where the only memory is of the war thirty years ago that turned the whole of life into a memory. And in this railroad station, where the only woman one could still love waits for the Transsiberian that will never take her anywhere. This world will not let us go. . . . You both are laughing as you hurry along there in your little circle of sunlight. But just wait. I know how to escape from it all. I know. . . .

I stopped for a moment. They were moving on, taking with them their aureole filled with ringing voices. I had a vision of the cedar trees with the big rusty nails. How close at hand it was, that final silence, that escape with no return. How good it was!

"You haven't even asked what we are going to do in the city, Juan!"

Samurai's voice rang out suddenly and roused me from my daydreams.

The seething mass of words I had so far been holding in exploded: "And what could you be doing? Going like feebleminded idiots to the post office to listen to the telephone operators: 'Please, who is the stupid fucker who wants to speak to Novosibirsk? Cabin number two!' Wow! Novosibirsk! You're already drooling at the thought of it, both of you!"

Instead of losing his temper, Samurai burst out laughing.

"Look, Utkin! The bear's waking up. Ha ha ha!"

Then, winking at his companion, he announced: "We are going to see . . . Belmondo!"

"Bel-*mon*-do," Utkin corrected him, laughing.

"No, Belmon-*do*! Shut up, Duckling. You don't know a thing about films."

It must have been the air of the taiga that had intoxicated them. For they began to laugh, to shout this incomprehensible word louder and louder, each one insisting on his own pronunciation. Samurai pushed Utkin and knocked him over, as he went on yelling those three resounding syllables. Utkin retaliated by throwing fistfuls of snow at Samurai's face.

"Belmon-*do*!"

"Bel-*mon*-do! In Italian it's Bel-*mon*-do. . . ."

"Is it a man or a woman?" I asked, dangerously serious, baffled by the neuter "o" ending.

Their laughter became torrential.

"Hey, Samurai! Just listen to him! If it's not a chick, he won't come with us! Ha ha ha!"

"Sure, sure, she's a woman, Juan! With a mustache . . . And with a . . . with a big . . . a big . . ." Samurai could not get to the end of his sentence.

They were laughing like madmen, crawling about on all fours, their feet tied in knots by their snowshoes, which they had not unfastened. The name rang out so strangely in the midst of the taiga. . . .

No doubt they thought their laughter had won me over. I let myself fall into the snow beside them, shaking my head frenetically and guffawing noisily. And it was the laughter that allowed me to weep all my drunkenness away. . . .

Then, when the last groans of our orgy had ceased, when we found ourselves, all three, stretched out across a sunlit clearing, our eyes filled with the sky, Samurai whispered in an enfeebled but vibrant voice: "Belmondo!"

≋ 2 ≋

≈ 8 ≈

It was the shark that saved me. . . .

I think if the film had begun differently I would have run out of the cinema and thrown myself under the wheels of the first truck that came by. In the deafening uproar of that brutal engine I would have sought out the blissful silence of the cedar tree. . . .

The film could so easily have begun with a shot of a woman walking through the streets while the credits roll — a woman "walking to meet her destiny." Or with one of a man at the wheel of his car, his impassive face hypnotizing the bemused spectators. Or even with a scenic panorama . . . But it was a shark.

Well, first we saw a man with a shifty face and a shabby light suit. A man trying to call someone from a telephone booth on the sunny promenade of a southern town. He kept glancing around anxiously, cupping his hand over the mouthpiece. He did not have much time. A helicopter appeared in the azure sky. . . . The machine stopped above the phone booth, lowered enormous claws, picked up the booth, and carried it off into the sky. Inside it the wretched spy was shaking the receiver, trying to pass on his ultrasecret message. . . . But the monstrous claws were already opening. The booth fell, plummeted into the sea, landed on the bottom, and there two frogmen secured it very adroitly to a long cage. Using up his last few mouthfuls of air, the spy turned toward the door of the cage. . . . He even managed to draw his pistol and fire. And produced a ridiculous stream of bubbles . . .

A splendid shark, which was, we guessed, ravenously hungry, darted into the submerged booth, pointing its snout at the spy's stomach. The water turned red. . . .

A few moments later Belmondo made his appearance. And the man who was evidently his boss was telling him about his colleague's tragic end. "We succeeded in recovering his remains," he said in very solemn tones. And he showed him a can of . . . shark's fin soup!

It was too silly! Gloriously silly! Completely improbable! Wonderfully crazy!

We had no words to express it. We simply had to accept it and experience it for what it was. Like an existence parallel to our own.

The feature film had been preceded by a newsreel. The three of us were sitting in the front row — the least popular of all, but there were no other seats left when we got there. The voice-over, both ingratiating and hectoring, was pouring out its commentary on the political events of the day. First we saw the imperial splendor of some hall in the Kremlin, where an old man in a dark suit was pinning a medal to the chest of another old man. "In recognition of the merits of Comrade Gromygin toward the fatherland and the people, and his contribution to the cause of international détente, and on the occasion of his seventy-fifth birthday," declaimed the voice-over in ringing tones. And the assembled dark suits began to applaud.

Next appeared a woman in a little polka-dot satin dress who was moving at an incredible speed amid hundreds of bobbins, all turning at maximum velocity. She broke off from her work for a moment just to declare in strident tones: "I'm currently operating a hundred and twenty looms. But to celebrate the seventieth anniversary of our beloved Party, I solemnly resolve to transfer to a hundred and fifty looms." And once again we saw her nimble fingers dancing between the threads and bobbins. Indeed, she now seemed to me to be running from one loom to the next faster than ever, as if she were already preparing to break the record. . . .

The lights came on again before being switched off for the feature film. Samurai nudged me with his elbow and offered me a handful of roasted sunflower seeds. I gripped them in my palm, while remaining in an opaque, all-enveloping torpor. She's going to operate a hundred and fifty looms, I was thinking. Then maybe a hundred and eighty. I sensed that this record-breaking weaver and the splendors of the Kremlin were mysteriously connected both to our dark district center and to the Transsiberian, with that red-haired woman forever waiting for it. . . . I also knew that as soon as the darkness returned I would fling my seeds to the ground and escape to that road shaken by the passage of giant trucks. Yes, from the moment of those opening scenes, there would be a woman walking to meet her destiny — or a man at the steering wheel of his car. . . .

But it was the shark! The absurdity of the can of fish soup containing the digested mortal remains of the spy was probably the only means by which I could have been kept on the fragile shores of life. Yes, what was needed was precisely that degree of harebrained madness for me to be snatched from reality and catapulted onto that sunny promenade, into that sunken cage where the mind-blowing execution was being prepared. The secret agent devoured by a shark and ending up in a can of fish soup was just what was needed.

And there were also women on that promenade. Above all, those two who for several seconds hid the telephone booth with their miniskirted silhouettes, their indolent bodies, their suntanned legs.

Oh, those divine legs! They moved around on the screen, in time with the sensual, swaying gait of those two shapely young creatures. Tanned thighs that seemed not to have the least idea of the presence, somewhere in the world, of winter, of Nerlug, of our Siberia. Or of the camp whose barbed-wire entanglements had ensnared the sun pendulum. These legs demonstrated with extreme persuasiveness — though without seeking to convert anyone at all — the possibility of an existence without the Kremlin, without weaving looms and other achievements of socialist emulation. Magnificently apolitical thighs. Serenely amoral. Thighs outside History. Apart from all ideology. Without any utilitarian ulterior motive. Thighs for thighs' sake. Quite simply beautiful tanned women's legs!

The shark and the apolitical thighs prepared the way for the appearance of our hero.

He came in many guises, like some Hindu divinity in its infinite incarnations. Now at the wheel of an endless white automobile hurtling into the sea, now making waves in a swimming pool with powerful butterfly strokes, attracting lustful looks from bathing beauties. He demolished his enemies in a thousand ways, fought his way out of the nets they flung over him, rescued his companions in arms. But above all, he seduced unremittingly.

Enthralled, I melted into the multicolored cloud of the screen. So, the woman was not unique!

With unconscious force, I was still gripping the fistful of sunflower seeds. They had become hot, and the blood throbbed in my clenched fist. As if it were my heart I was holding in my hand, so that it should not explode from too much emotion.

It was quite a different heart. Henceforth there was nothing final about the tragic night it had lived through. The red-haired woman's izba was being swiftly transformed, before my very eyes, into just an episode, an experience, one amorous adventure (the first) among many. Under cover of the darkness I turned my head slightly and, furtively, examined Samurai's and Utkin's profiles. This time I was observing them with a discreet and indulgent smile. With an air of worldly superiority. I felt so much closer to Belmondo than the two of them were, so much better informed about the secrets of feminine sensuality!

And on the screen, in a highly acrobatic but elegant manner, our hero was toppling a superb female spy, in an amorous clinch, onto some piece of furniture that looked quite unsuitable for love. . . . And the tropical night drew a conniving veil over their entwined bodies. . . .

With half-closed eyes, I inhaled deeply exotic scents that tickled the nostrils and made the eyes go misty.

I was saved.

On the whole, we understood little of the universe of Belmondo at the time of that first showing. I do not believe all the plot twists of this farcical parody of spy films could have been accessible to us. Nor the constant shuttling back and forth between the hero, a writer of adventure novels, and his double, the invincible secret agent, thanks to whom the novelist sublimates the miseries and frustrations of his personal life.

We had not grasped this rather obvious device at all. But we perceived the essential: the surprising freedom of this multiple world, where people seemed to escape those implacable laws that ruled our own lives, from the humblest workers' canteen to the imperial hall of the Kremlin, not forgetting the silhouettes of the watchtowers fixed over the camp.

Of course, these extraordinary people had their sufferings and their setbacks too. But the sufferings were not without remedy, and the setbacks stimulated fresh boldness. Their whole lives became an exuberant overreaching of themselves. Muscles were tensed and broke chains, the steely look rebuffed the aggressor; bullets were always delayed for a moment as they nailed the shadows of these leaping beings to the ground.

And Belmondo-the-novelist took this combative freedom to its symbolic apogee: the secret agent's car missed a turn and fell from a clifftop; but the unbridled imagination retrieved it at once by making it go into reverse. In this universe even the step over the brink was not terminal.

Generally the crowd of spectators dispersed quickly after evening performances. They would be in a hurry to dive into a dark alley, go home, get into bed.

This time it was quite different. People emerged slowly, at a sleepwalker's pace, a faint smile on their lips. Spilling out onto a little patch of waste ground behind the cinema, they spent a moment marking time, blinded, deafened. Intoxicated. They exchanged smiles. Strangers paired off, formed unaccustomed, fleeting circles, as in a very slow, agreeably irregular dance. And the stars in the milder sky seemed larger, closer.

It was under this light, less cold than before, that we walked along those little twisting alleys that had been reduced to narrow passageways between mountains of snow. We were on our way to the house of Utkin's grandfather, who let us stay in his big izba on our visits to the city.

Walking along Indian file in the depths of this maze of snow, we were silent. The universe we had just been exposed to remained, for the moment, beyond words. All there was to express it was the languid beauty of the night of the thaw, the quiet breathing of the taiga, these close stars, the denser color of the sky and the more vivid tones of the snows. But we could still only sense it in our flesh, in the quivering of our nostrils, in our young bodies, which drank in both the starry sky and the scents of the taiga. Filled to the brim with this new universe, we carried it in silence, afraid of spilling its magical contents. Only a repressed sigh escaped occasionally to convey this overload of emotions: "Belmondo . . ."

It was in Utkin's grandfather's izba that the eruption took place. We all began shouting at the same time, waving our arms and leaping around, each eager to portray the film in the most lively manner. We roared, as we struggled in the nets flung by our enemies; we snatched the glamorous creature from the sadistic clutches of the executioners as they prepared to cut off one of her breasts; we machine-gunned the walls before rolling onto a divan. We were at one and the same time the spy in the telephone booth and the shark pointing its aggressive snout, and even the can of fish soup!

We were transformed into a pyrotechnic display of gestures, grimaces, and yells. We were discovering the ineffable language of our new universe. That of Belmondo!

In any other circumstance, Utkin's grandfather, a man with the corpulence of a weary and melancholy giant, whose slow gait and white hair made him reminiscent of a polar bear, would have quickly rebuked us. But on this occasion he watched our triple performance in silence. The three of us together must have succeeded in re-creating the atmosphere of the film. Yes, he must have pictured the underground labyrinth lit by the dismal flames of torches, and the wall to which the glamorous martyr was chained. He saw a monstrous figure, squat and shriveled, cackling with perverse and impotent lust, as he drew closer to his scantily clad victim and raised a pitilessly glittering blade over her delectable breast. But a mingled roar came from our three outraged throats. The hero, triple in his strength and beauty, flexed his muscles, broke the chains, and flew to the aid of the gorgeous prisoner. . . .

The polar bear screwed up his eyes mischievously and left the room.

Samurai and I broke off our theatricals, thinking we had really offended Grandfather too much. Only Utkin remained in his actor's trance, shuddering as if it were he who risked losing a breast.

Grandfather reappeared in the room, grasping the neck of a bottle of champagne with his great knotty fingers. My eyes opened wide. Samurai uttered a resounding "Aha!" And Utkin emerged from his epileptic fit and summed up all our emotions in a single exclamation, still talking about the film: "Well, that's the West for you!"

Grandfather put three chipped china cups and a thick glass tumbler on the table.

"I've been saving this bottle for a friend," he explained, liberating the cork from the wire top. "But he, poor fellow, had the odd idea of dying in the meantime. He was a friend from the front. . . ."

We hardly heard his explanations. The cork leaped out with a joyful crack, there was a moment of cheerful urgency — abundant froth, fierce popping of bubbles, a white surge spilling onto the tablecloth. And finally the first mouthful of champagne, the very first in our lives . . .

It was only years later, thanks to that bitter clarification of the past that comes with age, that we would remember the friend from the front. . . . But on that evening of the thaw long ago there was only this icy tickling inside our scorched throats, which caused tears of joy to well up. A happy weariness like that of actors after a first night. And Utkin's summary, still ringing in our ears: "Well, that's the West for you!"

Yes, the Western World was born in the sparkle of Crimean champagne, in the middle of a big izba buried in the snow after a French film several years old.

It was the Western World at its most authentic, because

engendered in vitro. In that thick glass tumbler that had been washed by whole waves of vodka. And also in our virgin imaginations. In the crystalline purity of the air of the taiga.

It was there, the West. And that night we dreamed of it with open eyes in the bluish darkness of the izba. . . . And three shadowy figures appeared on that southern promenade, whom the summer visitors certainly will not have noticed. These three figures walked around a telephone booth, strolled past a café terrace, and, with their timid gaze, followed two young creatures with beautiful tanned legs. . . .

Our first steps in the Western World.

We were flying through the taiga, stretched out along the trunks of cedar trees on the trailer of a powerful tractor, like those that carried rockets in the army. The rough bark under our backs, the sky sparkling above our eyes, the silvery shadows of the forest on either side of the road. The sunny air inflated our sheepskin coats like sails and shot us through with the smell of resin.

It was strictly forbidden to transport people on trailers, especially when loaded. But the driver had accepted us with cheerful nonchalance. It was the first sign of the changes brought into our existence by Belmondo. . . .

The window of the cabin was lowered, so soft did the air seem that morning. And all along the road we could hear the driver telling the story of the film to his passenger, the foreman of the loggers. Lying flat out on the trees, we followed his narration, delivered with exclamations, oaths, and broad gestures, as his hands perilously left the steering wheel.

From time to time he uttered a particularly ringing cry. "He's got his first tooth, my boy! Ha ha ha! You know what I mean? That's it. My wife wrote to me. . . ."

And he resumed his narrative: "So then he pulls on the chains with all his strength, like that. . . . Sure thing, you could hear his bones cracking. Wow! And bingo! he chucks them in the air. And the other one, with his blade, was just a couple of steps away from the girl. And she — I can't tell you what a great pair of tits she's got. And this bastard wants to cut one of them off. You know what I mean? So the guy goes in right under him and ker-pow! No, no, don't worry. I'm holding the wheel."

And again he interrupted his story to proclaim his fatherly pride: "Hey, the little rascal! His first tooth . . . Milka writes: 'I can't feed him anymore — he bites my breast till it bleeds.' Ha ha ha! He's just like his dad."

The world seemed wonderfully transfigured. All we needed was a miracle to be finally convinced of it. And the miracle came.

It was close to the Devil's Bend, even more dangerous under the drifts from the snowstorm. At the place where we should have been moving cautiously, making a slow descent to the bank of the Olyei. But the story was reaching its culmination. . . .

The tractor with its heavy trailer hurtled down the slope, without even slowing down, and plunged out over the thin ice undermined by warm springs. . . .

There was a yell, quickly stifled, from inside the cabin; an oath uttered by Samurai. And then several apocalyptic and interminable seconds, filled with the creaking of the ice giving way under the wheels . . .

We came to ourselves a hundred yards farther along, already on the other bank. The driver stopped the engine and jumped out into the snow. His passenger followed him. The white surface of the river was incised by two black tracks that were slowly filling with water. . . .

In the absolute silence, nothing could be heard but a faint whistling coming from the engine. The sky had quite a new sparkle to it.

Later, no doubt, the driver and the foreman would talk about a crazy stroke of luck. Or about the speed of the tractor, which had been flying along, scarcely touching the ground. But without their admitting it to themselves, the ruins of the church on the highest part of the riverbank would come into their minds. And without knowing how to think about it, let alone talk about it, they would muse on that remote childish presence (the first tooth!). Maybe this had mysteriously sustained the heavy machine as it crossed the fragile ice. . . .

But we preferred to believe in a simple miracle; from now on this would be so natural in our lives.

On my return, everything in our izba seemed strange to me. It was the strangeness of familiar objects staring at me with curiosity; they seemed to be waiting for my first move. The day before yesterday I had left that room in the morning, to go to school. Since then there had been the switch operator's shanty; the station waiting room; the snowstorm; the house of the red-haired woman; the bridge; the truckdriver. . . . I shook my head, overcome with a singular dizziness. Yes, then my return across the snow-filled valley, the rusty nails of the hanged men . . .

My aunt came in, carrying the big kettle.

"I've made some pancakes, but some of them are burned; you can leave those," she said in her most normal voice, putting on the table a plate with a pile of golden pancakes.

I looked at this woman in perplexity. There she was entering the room, and she was coming from quite a different era. From before the snowstorm . . . Suddenly I remembered that there had been the sunny promenade beside the sea, the shark, the underground chamber with the chained beauty. . . . I felt myself reeling. Without explaining anything to my aunt, I left the room and pushed open the front door.

The evening sun was drowsing behind the castellated skyline of the taiga, caught in the watchtowers' invisible trap. Thanks to the purplish haze from the mild spell, you could stare at the coppery disk without screwing up your eyes. And the disk, I was sure, was swaying slightly above the barbed wire. . . .

Next day when Samurai knocked on our door and said to me with a wink: "Let's go!" there was no mistaking what he proposed.

We put on our snowshoes, collected Utkin close by his izba, and left Svetlaya. . . .

The city, twenty-three miles by road, was nineteen if you cut through the taiga. Eight hours on the march, plus a couple of stops to have a bite to eat and especially to give Utkin a breather. An entire day's journey. At the end of it: a sunset and the mists of the city that lay between two arms of the taiga, where it opened out gradually. And closer and closer came the hour, which each time became more magical: six-thirty P.M. The evening performance. Belmondo's.

Already the dense taiga was opening out; our snowy road was leading us straight to that promenade beside the sea and into the midst of that tanned crowd of extraterrestrials in the Western World. . . .

The first time, we had understood little. And indeed, there were things in the film it was hard for us to comprehend. The character of the publisher, for example. His relationship with our hero was an absolute mystery to us. Why was Belmondo afraid of this obese, inelegant man who hid his baldness under a wig? What dominion could he exercise over our superman and by what right? How dared he carelessly cast aside the manuscript that our hero brought him in his office?

For want of any credible explanation, we concluded it was sexual rivalry. And indeed, the hero's lovely neighbor was the target of repeated assaults by this monstrous literary bureaucrat. The whole audience held its breath when, drooling with lust, he feasted his prying eyes on the delectable backside of the young woman as she rashly leaned a little too far over the desk. And it was he who later pounced on the unfortunate woman, scattering his thick-lipped kisses all over her body when her defenses were down as a result of a treacherous drugged cigarette. . . .

Many of the nuances in this film escaped us. But thanks to our sixth sense, as young savages from the taiga, we could perceive intuitively what intellectually we could not know about the lives of Westerners. And we had decided to see the film ten or twenty times over if need be, but to understand everything! Everything down to the detail that tortured us for several days: when the lovely creature called on our hero, who was evidently a most welcoming host, why did she refuse his offer of a glass of whiskey?

≋ 9 ≋

WE SAW THE FILM seventeen times. In fact, we no longer watched it, we lived in it. Having once tiptoed our way warily onto the sunny promenade, we now set about exploring the most intimate nooks and crannies of this secret world. The plot was learned by heart. Now we could allow ourselves to study its surroundings and its backdrops: A piece of furniture in the hero's apartment — some little cupboard whose use was unknown, which the director himself very likely never noticed. A bend in the road, which the cameraman had framed without attaching the least importance to it. Or the reflection of a gray Parisian spring morning on the long thigh of the lovely neighbor, asleep half naked in front of our hero's door. Oh, that reflection! For us it became the eighth color of the rainbow, the one most necessary to the chromatic harmony of the world.

But above all, Belmondo . . . He embodied this whole complex repertoire of adventures, colors, passionate embraces, roars, leaps, kisses, breaking waves, musky scents, brushes with death. He was the key to this magic universe, its fulcrum, its engine. Its god . . .

We grasped the reason for his quicksilver performance. Indeed. He lived at this furious pace, embarking on a new action sequence before he had finished the last one, because he strove to achieve divine omnipresence. To bring together through his muscular and supple body all the elements of the universe. To become the very substance of their fusion. Like a human blender, he mixed an intoxicating cocktail from the dazzling spray of the waves, the sensual pulp of feminine bodies, lovers' panting, war cries, tropical languor, triumphant biceps, and a host of characters created with the titanic fecundity of the pagan gods: good, evil, droll, sensitive, eccentric, falsely tender, perverse, mythomaniac. . . .

He was a celestial clockmaker, who wound up the giant watch spring of this mind-blowing universe, set the southern sun and the languid stars on their courses. And his boxer's lungs breathed life into every soul that revolved around him. The carousel gathered speed, the cascading action sequences were transformed into a burlesque Niagara. And we were carried along on its torrent.

There were nevertheless times when our hero, while in full amorous and military cry, would suddenly stop and choose to be solitary, sad, misunderstood. Like a god in the midst of his creation when it no longer has need of him . . . Then a moment later he would fly off into the sky, attached to some fiery helicopter. But we who were tucked away in an obscure corner of his universe had glimpsed that moment of melancholy and solitude. . . .

The process of exploring the Western World continued, with its setbacks and its victories. One day we finally succeeded in defining the role of the publisher. He was classified: an evil man whose sexual appetite bore no relation to his physical and intellectual insignificance, a being who preyed on the noblest human gift, the capacity to dream.

This discovery coincided with another one, three or four showings later. We solved the mystery of the doubling of Belmondo!

The coming and going between the luxurious villas frequented by the master spy and the writer's modest apartment; between the athlete with a sunburned body and the slave to the typewriter who is more or less depressive and ravaged by nicotine addiction — this disconcerting alternation finally yielded its secret. And it was the glamorous spy who greatly assisted our investigation.

For she, too, was quite ambiguous. Chained to the wall of the underground chamber, she struggled; her struggling was highly provocative. Her tattered dress was on the brink of spilling out a magnificent breast into the lubricious palm of the transmogrified publisher. A superb breast, destined for a sadistic mastectomy. Her emerald eyes, admirably slanting, were those of a captured antelope. Her body had the aerodynamic curves of that noble animal. Her abundant hair rippled over her bare shoulders. The sadist approached, brandishing his blade, and we almost regretted that the hero's chains had yielded so quickly. Another moment, and the publisher-executioner would have stripped the marvelous antelope's body of those useless rags. . . .

It took us at least ten showings before we began to recognize the features of the antelope in the appearance of the rather pale student who lived in the same apartment building as the writer. This remote prototype for the glamorous spy, this pale shadow, was seen in a very humdrum setting of rainy days in Paris — a tall girl in jeans, her generous outlines erased, flattened out. A thick sweater camouflaged all hint of curves, eliminated all trace of sensuality. Her serious student's glasses dulled the sparkle in her eyes. And yet it was still she, our antelope with the shapely and muscular buttocks, our spy whose heaving bosom swelled full and round beneath the tatters of her dress.

Yes, it was she. But what a difference! The student in the Parisian rain seemed like an abortive double for the antelope of the tropical nights.

And it was by comparing this drab replica with the original that we glimpsed the secret of Western man's fantasies. Or rather those of the Western husband . . . The gorgeous antelope, the original — endowed with all possible physical charms — was his mistress, real or imagined. And the copy, devoid of all the sensual extras, was his wife. . . .

And how perspicacious our juvenile discovery was! Twenty years later, wandering through the capitals of the West, we would rediscover this erotic ambiguity that Belmondo had suggested to us. The women of male fantasies — on the covers of magazines or in red-light districts — would have breasts capable of tempting any sadistic publisher, and full golden thighs, like those of our fabulous antelope. While the wives would go on show with the bony angles of their shoulders, their nonexistent hips, and their flat chests. People would talk to us about the fashion, the style of the times, the puritan ideal, the equality of the sexes. But we would not be fooled. For we had explored that Western World of ours down to its murky subconscious depths!

Why Belmondo? Why in those long ago days at the time of the mild spell? In the blue dusk of February? At the six-thirty performance, when they generally showed long war films? In the Red October cinema, half buried in the snow?

What occurred was a veritable epidemic of Belmondophilia. A Belmondomania that had nothing in common with a passing infatuation for some Italian comedy or a fleeting craze for a Hollywood western. After the second performance the management of the Red October was compelled to put in an extra row of seats. We even saw one spectator sitting on a stool he had brought from home. . . . And the charm did not fade!

In the long waiting line, which almost matched that of the visitors to Lenin's tomb, we saw more and more unlikely people appearing. Two brothers Nerestov, renowned sable hunters who rarely came to the city — and then only to pour a fluid stream of furs from their bags . . . It was so strange to see them lining up in front of the ticket window among the citizens in their Sunday best. Their faces tanned by the icy wind; their enormous silver-fox fur shapkas; their curly beards: everything about them evoked their solitary life in the heart of the taiga. . . .

And then the legendary home distiller Sova, a robust and intrepid old woman, whom the militia had never managed to catch *in flagrante delicto*. She carried out her criminal activities, according to some people, in an abandoned mine, whose exit, half caved in, was hidden amid the gooseberry bushes in her garden. We always pictured her in the vaults of this gold mine, beneath the wooden supports, lit by the uncertain light of an oil lamp. A witch busy at her stills . . . This dark mine was only a step removed from the underground chamber with the beauty in chains, rescued by our hero. Old Sova took that step, her head held high, and came and sat down in the front row one day, dressed in her full brown sheepskin coat, with a monumental fox-fur hat on her head.

Yes, soon Belmondomania seemed like a powerful ground swell that brought surprising human species to the surface of our life. It was a surge that ran through the most remote villages, seeped into foresters' lodges, and, visibly, even shook the icy calm of the watchtowers. Each performance brought its surprises. . . .

One day I noticed that the seat next to me was empty. We always sat in the front row. No longer because we had arrived late, but in order to be alone face-to-face with Belmondo, to be able to make our way onto the sunlit promenade without having to step over heads and fox-fur hats . . . The empty seat on my left did not surprise me unduly at first. Someone had decided to come in after the newsreel, I thought, making use of those ten minutes of Kremlinian news to smoke a cigarette in the foyer. However, the newsreel — on this occasion, apart from the inevitable presentation of medals, we saw some marine fishermen who had overfulfilled the fishing plan by thirty percent — yes, the newsreel came to an end, the lights came on for a moment and then went off again, but the seat remained unoccupied. I was already preparing to move, as the empty seat seemed to me more centered. . . .

It was at that moment that the huge silhouette of a stooping man slipped across the screen, which was already ablaze with the brilliance of the south, and I felt one of his heavy boots stumbling against my feet in the darkness. The tardy spectator settled in his seat. Before the arrival of the helicopter above the telephone booth, I glanced at my neighbor. . . .

Recognizing him, I began slowly shrinking down between the armrests. I wanted to make myself very small, invisible, nonexistent.

For it was Gera. Gerassim Tugai was his real name. A name pronounced by all the inhabitants of the region in tones of nervous respect. He was the one who was "stealing gold from the state," in the opinion of my aunt and her friends. The one who was being frantically sought after by the militia and whom we had passed one summer's day in the heart of the taiga. The one who, hidden away in the wild and inaccessible depths, washed the gold-bearing sand of a little clear, fast-flowing river amid the silence of the centenarian cedar trees.

Overcoming my fear, I stared at him discreetly. His broad bearskin coat smelled of the fresh wind of the snowy spaces. His shapka, with earflaps tied at the back of his neck, was reminiscent of a great Nordic warrior's helmet. He sat in a proudly independent posture, his huge silhouette towering above the whole row of spectators.

The more I examined his profile by the changing and multicolored light of the screen, the more a strange resemblance emerged in his features. Yes, he reminded me of someone I knew very well. . . . But who? On his brow, a lock of hair escaped from below the shapka. . . . A flattened nose, the result of some brawl, no doubt. A determined set to his lips, a slightly carnivorous smile. A powerful, massive jaw. And that lively brown eye . . .

Dumbfounded and not daring to trust my intuition, I looked at the screen. Belmondo was emerging from the glittering azure of a swimming pool and settling into a deck chair beside the glamorous spy. I studied his profile. The lock of hair he tossed back from his wet brow, his nose, his lips. His eyes . . . I turned toward my neighbor. Then toward the screen. And once again toward the man in the bearskin . . .

Yes, it was he. There are no explanations for magic. Nor did I try to understand. I remained in a strange zone between-two-worlds, between these two perfectly similar faces, brought together within the alchemist's distilling flask that the dark space of the Red October cinema had become. In the midst of a slow transmutation of the real into something more true and more beautiful . . .

I came to my senses with a start. My neighbor's great boots had caught on my feet in passing. He was leaving the auditorium one or two minutes before the end. The glass flask was shattered. I almost ran after him, whispering: "Wait, you're going to miss the best scene in the film!" It was the one in which the lovely neighbor was asleep outside the hero's door, revealing her long thigh that was the eighth color of the rainbow. . . .

I did not run. I did not call out. We could hear the side door softly closing. The man in the bearskin had disappeared. . . .

When the lights came on among the slow-moving, dazzled, and smiling crowd we could see two uniformed officers. Their epaulets were colored crimson, the distinctive insignia of the units that guarded the camp. The spectators gave them amused, furtive looks, as much as to say: "Aha! You, too . . ."

Yes, they, too, had spent time in the magic flask. Alongside the redoubtable Gera . . .

I never spoke about him to Samurai or Utkin. They would doubtless have laughed in my face. But after that strange evening I have come to realize that magic is broken precisely because man dares neither speak of it nor believe in it. He shows himself unworthy of miracles by trying to reduce them to some banal material cause.

Besides, during the time of that mild weather one miracle more or less was not an issue. The day after the mysterious appearance of the man in the bearskin, whom should we see in the waiting line but . . . Utkin's grandfather! He looked quite embarrassed, like an adult caught red-handed in some piece of childishness. And he hastened to justify himself: "Well, what do you expect? The whole world talks of nothing else. . . . A friend of mine who's a doctor told me one of his patients asked him to delay his operation so that he could go and see this film. So I thought . . ."

And to exonerate himself he paid for all four tickets.

Why Belmondo?

With his flattened nose, he looked like many of us. Our life — taiga, vodka, camps — sculpted faces of this type. Faces with a barbaric beauty that shone through the roughness of their tortured features.

Why him? Because he waited for us. He did not abandon us

on the threshold of some luxurious palace, but — thanks to the coming and going between his dreams and his ordinary life — he was always at our side. We could follow him into the unimaginable.

We also loved him for the magnificent uselessness of his exploits. For the joyful absurdity of his triumphs and his conquests. The world we inhabited was based on the crushing inevitability of the radiant future. We were all conscripted into this logic — the weaver darting between her hundred and fifty looms, the marine fisherman trawling the fourteen seas of the empire, the loggers undertaking to cut down more each year. This irresistible progress defined the object of our presence on this planet. The awarding of decorations at the Kremlin was the supreme symbol of it. And even the camp found its place in this planned harmony — a place was certainly needed for those who showed themselves to be temporarily unworthy of the great project, for the inevitable dross of our paradisal existence.

But now came Belmondo with his pointless exploits, his achievements with no purpose, his gratuitous heroism. We saw a strength that took pride in itself with no thought for the result; the gleam of muscles that were not concerned to break productivity records. We discovered that the physical presence of a man could be beautiful in itself! Without any ulterior motive, be it messianic, ideological, or futurist. From now on we had a name for this marvelous "in itself": Western World.

And then there was also that encounter at the airport. The spy who was to meet our hero had to have about her person an agreed object, an identifying sign. And it was a . . . *karavai,* a loaf of black bread, Russian — you can't get more Russian than that — and called by its Russian name in a French film! A shout of delight and national pride ran through the rows at the Red October cinema. . . . On the way back to Svetlaya this time we spoke of nothing else: so over there in the Western World they did have an inkling that we existed!

Why Belmondo?

Because he arrived at the right moment. He erupted in the midst of the snowbound taiga as if propelled there by a fantastic film stunt. Yes, it was one of his action sequences — a dazzling series of leaps, chases, pistol shots and fisticuffs, falls, spins of the steering wheel, takeoffs and touchdowns. That was how he had touched down in the midst of the taiga!

He arrived at the moment when the discontinuity between the promised future and our own present was on the brink of making us irremediably schizophrenic. When in the name of our messianic project the fishermen were preparing to leave not one single fish in the seas, and the loggers to transform the taiga into a desert of ice. While back in the Kremlin one old man was decorating another and anointing him "three times Hero of Socialist Labor" and "four times Hero of the Soviet Union," and there was no space left on the shrunken chest of the decorated person for all those gold stars . . .

When Belmondo took Siberia by storm, all that was part of it. The Kremlin; the hundred and fifty weaving looms; vodka as the sole means to combat the schizophrenic rupture between the future and the present. Not to mention the disk of the setting sun trapped in the barbed wire . . .

He leaped from a helicopter hooked onto the end of the Siberian sky, rolled in the snow, and erupted on the screen, inviting us to follow him. . . . It was a stroll beside the warm sea. By constantly turning our backs on the distant silhouette of the radiant future, we advanced gingerly into that terra incognita: the Western World.

But more than anything else: it was love. . . .

What did I know of it, what did any of the audience know

of it, before his arrival? We knew there was I've-had-her love. The most common currency in the emotional life of our rough country. And eternally-waiting-by-the-ferry love . . . And there was another kind, the one we generally encountered on the screen at the Red October. I recall one very typical film about love. . . .

Boy meets girl. On a path in the midst of the fields of rye, in the evening. They walk along silently, artistically shy, heaving eloquent sighs from time to time. The moment of decision approaches. The audience holds still, subsides, waiting for an appropriate embrace. The young kolkhoznik removes his cap, makes a broad circular gesture, and declares: "You know the rye this year, Masha: I bet it yields twelve quintals per hectare!"

A groan of frustration shook the darkened auditorium.

Especially because the heroine was very beautiful and her partner definitely virile. If her dress had been ripped into tatters, we would have been able to gaze at breasts just as well rounded as the one Belmondo's ravishing prisoner was in danger of losing. If she had lain down in the grass — which the whole auditorium was ardently longing for — then the shapeliness of her thighs would easily have rivaled the sensual curves of the spy. . . .

But all the lovers could see, hovering over the fields in the evening, was the misty outline of the messianic project, the sunbathed peaks of the future. They stifled their natural urges and concentrated on talking about the harvest. . . . The kiss came as a more or less optional extra. It made the screen go dark. And before it lit up again we heard the first wails of the baby that had appeared in the arms of its happy mother. Clearly these moments of darkness were a filmic expression of the night of the gestation period. . . .

The gulf between this official modesty and I've-had-her love was the same as that which lay between the prophetic future and Nerlug in the present. And at the bottom of this chasm was the house of the red-haired prostitute. A woman with a heavy, weary body. A woman who weeps as she lays out on a blanket photos with the edges carefully trimmed. Heaven knows why. Showing them to an adolescent who can only think of that dead bird within him — his dream of love. At the bottom of this chasm was that night of snowstorm and the Transsiberian backtracking. The washed-out face of the woman above the candle flame and her fingers caressing my hair . . .

Belmondo held out his hand to this adolescent with a dead bird nestling close to his heart. He drew him toward the southern sun. And the terrifying and unspeakable lava of love found words to speak its name with Western clarity: seduction, desire, conquest, sex, eroticism, passion. Like a true professional in love, he even included in his analysis the possible setbacks and disappointments that lie in wait for the young seducer in the early stages of his adventure. We saw him preparing a candlelit dinner to which he had invited his neighbor. He put on a dark suit, went on waiting and . . . fell asleep in the posture of a vanquished gladiator. She never came. . . .

Yes, the leap into the abyss of love was also an element in his storming of Siberia. And so that there should be no doubt on this subject, he had come and sat down beside me, disguised as Gerassim Tugai, in the front row of the Red October cinema. . . .

The thaw lasted only a few days. The winter took its revenge on this luminous interlude and brought a stinging polar wind, froze the stars in the black crystal of the sky.

But Belmondo fought back. On every free day or, as often as not, missing our classes at school, we woke up before sunrise and set off for the city. For the fourteenth time, the fifteenth, the sixteenth . . . We did not tire.

≈ 10 ≈

IN THE FOREST it was still night. The snow was sometimes gilded by the moon, sometimes intensely blue. Every young pine tree seemed like an animal lying in wait, every shadow was alive and watching us. We spoke little, not daring to break the solemn silence of this sleeping kingdom. From time to time a pine branch shook off a great white cap of snow. We heard the muffled rustling, then the stifled sound of it falling. And for a long time afterward crystals would flutter down beneath this awakened branch, iridescent green, blue, and mauve spangles. And everything became still again in the dreamy silver light of the moon. . . . Sometimes we heard a light rustling, while all the branches remained motionless. We pricked up our ears: "Wolves?" And above the clearing we saw the shadow of an owl passing. The silence was so pure that we seemed to feel the density and the suppleness of the icy air as the great gray wings of the bird cut into it.

It was during those still-shadowy hours of night that I liked to return to my secret. . . .

My companions were traveling through the forest to go and see a comedy, to learn some more dialogue by heart, to laugh. If I was on my way to the Red October, it was to participate in a miraculous transfiguration: soon I was going to have another body, another soul; and the bird in my breast was going to dance around my heart, fluffing out its feathers. But for the moment it did not stir. And with mournful relish I bore my adult grief within me — the house of the red-haired woman.

I believed my sorrow to be unique, just like the transfiguration that awaited me in the promised land of the Western World. And I would have been quite astonished to learn that Samurai and Utkin, as they slipped through the sleeping taiga, also carried beneath their sheepskin coats a grief and a hope. An enigma. A mysterious past. I was not the only member of the elect. . . .

The mystery surrounding Samurai was harsh and simple. He confided it to me one winter's evening a month before the arrival of our hero. We were in our little izba bathhouse, he in his copper tub, I stretched out on the hot, humid wood of the bench. Gusts of wind were peppering the tiny window with the dry snow that the great frosts bring. Samurai remained silent for a long time, then he began talking in a tone of assumed jocularity. As you do when recounting some childhood escapade. But it was palpable that at any moment his nonchalant voice was in danger of lurching into a stifled cry of pain. . . .

He must have been ten years old at the time. On a hot day in July, one of those scorching days in the continental summer, Samurai — who had not yet been nicknamed Samurai — came running out of the water. Quite naked, shivering under the baking sun. The river never became any warmer during those few weeks of midsummer heat.

He came out and ran toward the bushes where he had hung his clothes. Suddenly, stumbling against a stone or a thick root, he fell. He had no time to grasp that it was not a root: he had been cunningly tripped. Two hands gripped his waist. On all fours, he made an attempt to get away, still suspecting nothing. At the same moment he saw leather boots in front of him, felt the weight of a hand seizing his wet hair. He let out a cry. Then the one who had been squeezing his haunches began to punch him in the kidneys. Samurai arched his back, groaned, tried to escape again. But the heavy hand that was gripping his hair now fastened itself around his face like a muzzle. Two fingers with flat yellow nails were thrust into the base of his eye sockets — it was a threat: "One more shout and I'll poke your eyes out." However, he had time to notice that the man in front of him had knelt down. He heard several oaths and some rather nervous sniggering. Samurai did not understand why, if they wanted to kill him, they were so slow in producing a knife or a pike. . . . It seemed as if the one who was behind him was trying to tear his naked body in two by pulling his wet legs apart. Samurai cried out in pain, and in a momentary glimpse, which would remain with him, he saw that one of his attackers was starting to unbutton his pants. . . .

When danger threatens, a child reverts more readily to being the animal that is not yet wholly dormant within it. Only the agility of this animal saved Samurai. His body performed a series of movements of a rapidity beyond human perception. They were not so much actions as an electric vibration that ran through his body from his head to his feet. His arm threw off the hand muzzling him at the very instant when he raised his head slightly to weaken the pressure of the fingers in his eyes. His foot, abruptly lifted, went into the belly of his aggressor. His shoulder touched the grass, dragging his vibrating body toward the river . . .

But his transformation into a young animal caught in a trap had not been quite complete. At the last moment something in his back seemed to give way. A searing pain ran through it to the base of his skull. Samurai thought he would not be able to move another step. Once he had plunged into the water, however, the pain left him. As if the cold and supple stream had put everything back in place in his tortured young body . . .

He found himself on the opposite bank. He stared at the river with stupefaction. He had never before swum the Olyei. Too wide, too fast. He could not feel his body, could not distinguish between his own breathing and the respiration of the cedar trees. His soaked head was humming, melting into the luminous sky. And somewhere in the midst of this organism, without beginning or end, dissipated within the immensity of the taiga, could be heard the repeated, resonant calling of a cuckoo. . . .

On the opposite bank Samurai saw nobody. He waited until evening before returning. This time he swam holding on to a floating tree trunk. The Olyei was once more becoming impossible to cross. His clothes had not been touched. There were several cigarette butts scattered on the trampled ground. . . .

From that day forth Samurai became obsessed by strength.

Before that the world had been good. And simple. Like the tranquil luminosity of those white clouds in the sky and their reflection in the living mirror of the Olyei. But now there was this viscous stuff that lay stagnating in the dark pores of life, which were masked by words, by smiles. This was strength. At any moment it could overwhelm you, crush you against the ground, break you in half.

Samurai started to hate the strong. And in order to be able to resist them, he decided to harden his body. He wanted the animal agility that had saved him to become completely natural. . . .

By the autumn he could cross the river and back without resting. Hurling ourselves stark naked into the snow on emerging from the baths under the icy sky was his idea. In the beginning it was simply a military exercise. . . . He also knew that one must harden the edge of the hand. As the Japanese did. Soon he was breaking thick dry branches at the first blow. At the age of thirteen he had the strength of an adult man. He did not yet have the endurance. He often arrived at school with his face covered in bruises, his finger joints raw. But he was smiling. He was no longer afraid of the strong.

Then one day he swapped a tiny gold nugget (we all had a few nuggets) for a colorful foreign postcard. The glossy picture showed a blue sea, an avenue lined with palm trees and white houses with big windows. This was Cuba. The newspapers were constantly speaking of this country and of its people, who had the courage to resist the might of the United States. His hatred of the strong found its global target: Samurai fell in love with the little island and detested the Americans. His romantic attachment was embodied in a feminine figure he dreamed of: a beautiful companion in arms, a young woman fighter with Creole comeliness, who wore a combat uniform with rolled-up sleeves. . . .

But this love, just like the hatred, came too late. Revolutionary fervor was a thing of the past, and even in the depths of our Siberia they were beginning to make open fun of our old bearded friend. Likewise of Samurai, whose passion was known to everyone. The boys at school often sang for his benefit a jingle that had become very popular. It went to the tune of Castro's heroic "Barbudos" song, but the words were all different, tampered with:

Cuba, give us back our wheat.
Give us back our vodka too.
Your sugar's wet — and not too sweet.
Fidel, take it back, fuck you!

Samurai looked at them with disdain. The insolence of the weak was a puzzle: these mockers knew that he would not condescend to give them a hiding. . . . But deep inside, Samurai was troubled by a lot of embarrassing questions. Especially after the day when he received the ultimate blow below the belt from History.

It came at the end of a geography lesson. That day the teacher was talking about Central America. When the bell rang and the classroom emptied, Samurai walked up to the desk and took the colorful postcard with the view of Havana out of his bag. The azure sea, the palm trees, the white villas, the tanned strollers. The teacher studied it, then, turning it over, read the caption.

"Ah, of course," he confirmed. "But that was before the revolution! I was wondering. . . ."

He fell silent, then handed the card back to Samurai and explained, turning away: "You know, they are in a rather difficult economic situation. . . . Without our aid it would be really tough. An old friend of mine worked there as a volunteer. He says that even socks are rationed, one pair a year per person. . . . Of course, it's the imperialist blockade that causes that. . . ."

Samurai was stunned. So one must picture the bold "barbudos," their automatic rifles in their hands, waiting in line to get a new pair of socks!

When Belmondo arrived, Samurai was sixteen. All the wretched questions provoked by his disillusioned love were in the process of turning into a trauma that prevented him from seeing, breathing, smiling. He had become strong, but the evil that he set out to combat renewed itself like the heads of the Hydra. With the arrival of a new team of loggers; with a new drunken brawl on the steps of the liquor store. At the very most, all he had managed to conquer was a narrow zone of security around his own person. Life did not change. And the fair companion in arms, in her khaki pants and her combat jacket with rolled-up sleeves, had not yet shown up.

While the Yankee blue jeans that had made their appearance on the chubby legs of a local apparatchik's son were wreaking havoc among the hearts of the local Siberian maidens . . .

So should he go on breaking branches with the edge of his hand? Crossing the river while holding an iron bar above his head, a substitute for a future automatic rifle? Rebuking drunken loggers? Cutting off the Hydra's heads and doubling the evil? Living as if on a blockaded island? Defending weak people, who then hurl their perfidious mockery at your back?

It was then that Samurai encountered Belmondo. He witnessed his pointless feats, his fight for fight's sake. He discovered that to take up arms could be beautiful. That landing a blow could have its elegance. That the gesture was often worth more than the effort's objective. That what counted was panache.

Samurai was discovering the bitter aesthetic of the desperate struggle against evil. He saw it as the only way out of the labyrinth of awkward questions. Yes, to take up arms, thinking only of the beauty of the combat! To hurl oneself as a single trooper into the action sequence of war. And to quit the field of battle before the grateful weak can come and praise you to the skies or reproach you for any excesses. Yes, to fight, knowing that victory would be short-lived. Like in the film . . . Though the publisher was vanquished, turned into a laughingstock, and lost his wig, he would soon return to his inaccessible office. But the beauty of those last few moments would be the hero's best reward. Embracing his lovely neighbor — now won back — he leans over the balcony and hurls the pages of his manuscript at the retreating publisher and his clique. What madness, but what a gesture!

A week after the first showing Samurai had a fight with two drunken truckers in the workers' canteen. All the conventions were respected in this classic barroom scenario. The strident shrieking of the canteen woman; the silence of the human herd gripped both by fear and by the reflex "It's got nothing to do with me." And the young male lead who rises to his feet at the end of the room and walks toward the two aggressors. The truckers were newcomers; they did not know that this young man's hand broke thick branches at the first blow. Two or three lunges from his hand-sword sufficed to evict them. But Samurai could no longer be content for the scene to end like that. He went back into the canteen. Watched by the diners, rigid in front of their plates, he put down a crumpled ruble note in front of the cashier, as she cowered behind her counter, and remarked: "Those miserable wretches forgot to pay for their soup."

Then he strode out into the icy wind, accompanied by a buzz of admiration. . . .

Back home, he sat down in front of a mirror and stared at himself for a long time. A lock of dark hair fell across his brow; his nose was slightly squashed — the relic of some unequal combat; his lips were tensed in a determined line; a heavy lower jaw was accustomed to taking cannonball blows from the weighty fists of men. He gave a friendly wink at the face looking back at him out of the mirror. He had recognized him. He had recognized himself. . . . Never had our fabled Western World seemed so close!

11

THE SUN WAS RISING as we came out of the taiga, heading for the valley of the Olyei. As if we were leaving the night behind us deep inside that sleeping kingdom of pine trees, where the great owl glided through the silvery shadows, seeking a refuge for the daylight hours.

The red disk appeared from behind a cold veil and slowly replaced the gray and blue tones with shades of pink. Shaking off our nocturnal torpor, we began to talk, to exchange impressions of the last performance. But above all, to the point of exhaustion and of losing our voices, to imitate Belmondo . . .

This time, on our sixteenth trip to see the film, Samurai went ahead of us a little, striking out with long strides over the plain, whose smooth mauve surface was so inviting. I stopped to wait for Utkin. As he left the shadows of the forest and emerged onto this great, luminous space, he swung around the tip of a small pine tree buried under the snow and came to join me.

His gaze always used to make me feel a bit uneasy. The mixture of jealousy, despair, and resignation with which he surveyed my face . . .

This time there was none of it. Dragging his injured leg, he came up to me, his right shoulder pointing toward the sky, and smiled. He looked at me squarely like an equal, with neither bitterness nor jealousy. His duckling's gait seemed no longer to preoccupy him. I was struck by the serenity of his face. As I set off again, I told myself that I had been seeing these calm and somehow wiser eyes for some time now. I slowed my speed somewhat, allowing myself to be overtaken. Replying absentmindedly to the remarks of my companions, I began to think about the mystery surrounding Utkin.

For he, too, saw the six-thirty performance as much more than a simple burlesque comedy. . . .

On that spring day long ago when his body had been crushed by the ice floes in the thaw, his child's eyes had undergone a change of vision. In that instant Utkin had acquired a particular view of things such as only extreme pain or pleasure can bestow. At these moments we can observe ourselves — from a distance — as a stranger. A stranger unrecognizable in his overwhelming pain or in the spasms of extreme pleasure. For a few seconds we sustain this division into two. . . .

Utkin had seen himself that way. Against the pale wall of a hospital room. His suffering was so great that he was on the brink of asking himself: "But who is he, this thin little fellow, moaning and shivering in his plaster shell?" Yes, it was very early, at the age of eleven, that he experienced this perception. The maimed body crying out, suffering; and alongside it, it's hard to know exactly where, the detached, calm scrutiny. A bitter and serene presence. Like a bright autumn day, with the penetrating smell of dead leaves. Utkin knew this presence was also himself: a part of him. Perhaps the most important part. In any case, the most free. He could not have expressed the significance to himself of this division into two. But intuitively he perceived within him the tonality of that imaginary autumn moment. . . .

It was enough to close your eyes, put yourself in tune with the low sun gleaming in the yellow leaves; with the pure scent of the forest; with the limpid air . . . and you could pose the question, calm, disinterested: "But who is he, that little fellow dragging his lame leg along, pointing one shoulder toward the sky?"

Utkin loved to enter into that day which he had never seen, to dwell there amid the unknown trees with broad indented leaves, yellow and red, such as were not to be found in the taiga. To peer through this sun-drenched foliage at the little fellow as he limped along, his head bowed under the snow squalls . . .

The mystery of Utkin . . . The crux of it was that the huge triangle of ice that had suddenly become detached from the banks of the mighty river had left him enough time to realize what was happening. He had time to be aware of the gawking crowd, which drew back when they detected the ominous creaking; time to hear their shouts. And to be afraid. And to understand that he was afraid. And to try to save himself without making the human herd laugh at him as he jumped. And to realize that it was stupid to care about the laughter of the others. And to think: This is me, yes, this really is me; I am alone on this ice, which is breaking up, overturning into the flood; this is me; that's the sun; it is spring; I'm afraid.

Like a crystal that is marked with the incrustations of impurities, his grief would always retain this patina of feverish and banal thoughts. They would be engraved in the crystal, in its transparency of frozen tears.

The river was too powerful, its breathing was too slow, even at the moment of breakup, for the calamity to be sudden. The boy's eyes experienced it as if in slow motion. The man who risked being crushed by the ice himself and grabbed Utkin cried out cheerfully: "Just look at this drowned duckling! A bit further and he'd have gone in the drink. . . . Look, he's a regular duckling!"

He went on, uttering little laughs, so as to hide his own fear and reassure the gawking crowd. Utkin, who at this moment was becoming Utkin the Duckling, was sitting on the snow, hunched into a damp ball. He looked at the man laughing and wiping his raw hands on his pants. He looked at him with his blurred eye, benefiting from the last moments before the pain swept over him. In an inexpressible premonition, he sensed that this laughter already belonged to quite another period of his life. Likewise the encouraging remarks from the onlookers, as they wondered whether an ambulance should be called or if the Duckling would recover unaided, after drying himself and drinking some hot tea. The sun, too, was a sun from other days. Like the beauty of the spring. And this nickname he had just been given — Utkin — had been given to a being who no longer existed: a boy like any other, who had come to look at the thaw on this very ordinary morning of his life. . . .

And when, suddenly, the snow turned quite black, when the sun began to resonate and quiver and to penetrate into the burning mass that was his body, when the furrows of the first waves of pain began to lash his face, Utkin for the first time heard that distant voice: "But who is he, that little fellow shouting with pain, spitting up blood from his crushed lungs and twitching in the melted snow like a young bird with broken wings?"

The fact that the calamity had occurred without haste, in rhythm with the mighty river and the immensity of the ice blocks, impelled Utkin toward a reflection that was strange and very remote from any idea he had had as a child. He began to doubt the reality of everything that surrounded him. To doubt reality itself . . .

This doubt arose on the day when they took him home from

the hospital. Utkin was sitting in the room in their izba, a very clean room filled with friendly objects, each of which evoked faint echoes of memory, a room that had the gentle tonality of his mother's presence. His mother brought a kettle from the kitchen, placed two cups on the table, made the tea. And Utkin already knew that his life would never again be the same. That from now on the world would come to meet him, mimicking the lunges of his limping gait. That the whirligig of his schoolfellows' games would always fling him away from the center toward the periphery, toward inaction. Toward exclusion. Toward nonexistence. He knew that his mother would always have that assumed intonation in her voice and that somber glint of despair in her eyes, which no tenderness would be able to hide.

Once more he recalled that slow-motion calamity — the weighty and majestic advance of the ice floes, their titanic collision, the deafening sound of the impact, the piling up of the enormous fragments, revealing blocks of a greenish transparency, more than a yard thick. With infallible precision, his memory played back the syncopated sequence of his thoughts. Standing on the triangle of ice, scrabbling to reach an impossible equilibrium, he was afraid of others laughing at him. . . . And it was no doubt this fear of ridicule that made him clumsy. . . .

Yes, it had all turned on so little. If he had been a trifle quicker, slightly less embarrassed by the stares of the crowd massed on the riverbank, things would not have changed. If he had drawn back from the water's edge by a couple of inches, the tea he was about to drink with his mother could have had quite a different taste, and the spring day outside the windows quite a different meaning. Yes, reality would not have changed.

Dumbfounded, he was discovering that the solid, visible world regulated by adults who knew everything was suddenly proving to be fragile, improbable. A couple of inches more, a few mocking looks received, and you find yourself in a quite different dimension, in another life. A life where the comrades of yesterday run away and leave you limping in the melting snow, where your mother makes a superhuman effort to smile, where little by little people get used to the fact that this is how you are, and fix you once and for all with this new appearance.

This universe, suddenly uncertain, terrified him. But sometimes, without being able to express it clearly, Utkin experienced a heady freedom when he thought about the discovery he had made. It was that all these people took the world seriously, convinced by its appearance. And only he knew that all it needed was a small thing to render this universe unrecognizable.

It was then that he began to make visits to that sunlit autumn that he had never lived through, among broad yellow leaves that he had never seen. He could not even tell how that day came to be born in him. But it was born. Utkin closed his eyes and breathed the strong, fresh scent of the foliage. . . . From time to time an unpleasant whisper began to hiss in his head: "This day is not real, and the reality is that you are a cripple nobody wants to play with." Utkin did not know what to reply to this voice. Unconsciously he sensed that a reality that depended on a couple of inches and a few titters from gawking onlookers was more unreal than any dream. Not being able to say this, Utkin smiled and gazed with screwed-up eyes into the low sun of his autumn day. The air was translucent, the gossamer threads floated, swaying gently. . . . And this beauty was his best argument.

And then one day — he was already thirteen, two years into his new life — his grandfather gave him a story to read. His grandfather, that taciturn and solitary polar bear, had been a journalist. His text, two and a half typewritten pages, bore the indelible stamp of the journalistic style, almost as tenacious as the letter *k* in his typescript, which always jumped up higher than the others. But Utkin did not even notice these details in the text, he was so overwhelmed by the story. And yet in this story there was nothing unusual.

Like a reporter in the country of his youth, his grandfather conjured up a column of soldiers lost in the mire somewhere on the roads of the war in the icy November rain. Their army beaten, scattered, retreating before the advance of the German divisions, seeking refuge closer to the heart of Russia . . . The bare forests, the dead villages, the mud . . .

"Each soldier carried within him the memory of some beloved face, but I had no one. No girlfriend: I believed I was ugly and was very shy. No fiancée: I was also very young. No parents: destiny had wanted it that way. No one I could think about. I was as alone as you can be under the low, gray sky. From time to time a farm cart overtook our column. A thin horse, a pile of trunks, several frightened faces. For them we were the soldiers of defeat. One day we met a farm wagon in open country. A rainy dusk, wind, the road churned up. I was walking behind the others. There was no longer any order in our ranks. A woman with a baby in her arms lifted her face as if to bid us good-bye. Her eyes met mine for a moment. . . . Night fell and we were still marching. I did not yet know that I would remember for the rest of my life the look she gave me. In the war. Then in the camp for seven long years. And even today . . . Marching along in the dusk, I said to myself: 'At night to each of them comes a memory within him. And now I have the look she gave me.' . . . An illusion? A fantasy? Maybe . . . But thanks to that illusion I have come through hell. Yes, if I am alive, it is thanks to that look. That haven where the bullets could not touch me, where the boots of the guards bruising my ribs could not reach my heart . . ."

Utkin read and reread this tale, recounted it to himself several times. And one day, returning to his own simple story, he thought: But if what happened to me hadn't happened, I should never have understood what it meant, that look a soldier carried in his eyes all through the long night of the war. . . .

Utkin was sure of his luminous autumn day. But a man was

already awakening within this adolescent's body, within this frail, crippled shell. The world was exuding its sweet-tasting springtime poison, the mortal amber of love, the lava of female bodies. Utkin would have liked to take wing and join us, those of us who were already soaring in these intoxicating emanations. But his upthrust was shattered, his takeoff hurled him down toward the ground.

He was the same age as me, fourteen, during that memorable winter. At the time of his calamity and for some time afterward the female part of the school had paid a particular attention to him. The maternal instinct toward an injured child. But very soon his condition was accepted as normal, therefore of no interest. These little girls, from being future mothers who could love him as a sick doll, were turning into future fiancées. Utkin no longer interested them.

It was then that I began to intercept the look that he focused on my face: a mixture of jealousy, hatred, and despair. A silent but harrowing interrogation. And when, on the occasion of our swim, the two young women strangers observed us naked, Samurai and me, particularly me, through the dance of the flames, I understood that the intensity of this interrogation could one day be the death of Utkin.

But then came Belmondo . . . and as we went to see his film for the sixteenth time and Utkin emerged from the purplish shadow of the taiga, he took several steps toward me, regarding me with a dreamy smile, as if he had just awakened in the midst of this snowy plain lit by the mauve haze of the morning sun. And in his eyes I could find no unhealthy hostility. His faint smile seemed to be his response to the earlier interrogation. He waved his arm, gesturing at Samurai, who was pressing on a hundred yards ahead of us. He laughed softly: "What's got into him? Does he want to see more female spies than the rest of us?"

We speeded up a bit, to catch up with Samurai. . . .

Yes, one day came Belmondo. . . . And Utkin saw that his suffering and the interrogation that went unanswered had long since found classic expression in the Western World: the dreariness of so-called real life versus the pyrotechnics of fantasy; ordinary life and dreams. And Utkin fell in love with the poor slave to the typewriter. This was the Belmondo he felt close to. The one who climbed the stairs painfully, pumping his broken-winded lungs, ravaged by tobacco. In short, that very vulnerable being. Now hurt by his own son's boorishness; now by the unintended betrayal of his lovely young neighbor . . .

Yet it was enough for there to be a sheet of white paper in his machine, and reality was transfigured. The tropical night, thanks to the magic philter of its scents, made him strong; as swift as the bullets from his revolver; irresistible. And he never tired of moving back and forth between his two worlds, so as to unite them, in the end, with his titanic energy. The pages of typescript fluttered over the courtyard, and the lovely neighbor embraced this rather unheroic hero. In this happy ending Utkin saw a hope beyond words.

Now when he was climbing the high staircase at school, painfully dragging his foot, he pictured himself as that writer dogged by the misfortunes of daily life, that Belmondo of the rainy days. In the film, however, at the top of the staircase there was the pretty neighbor brimming with friendly concern. Whereas at school, in the passing throng of mocking faces, nobody was waiting for Utkin on the landing. "Life is stupid," a bitter voice said inside him, "stupid and cruel." "But there's always Belmondo," murmured another. . . .

Halfway on our journey, in the midst of the highway, bathed in sunshine, we stopped to have a bite to eat. The wind blowing along the valley was bitter. We looked for shelter and settled ourselves under the lee of a snow dune shaped by the storm. The icy blast passed right over its sharp-edged cornice. The day seemed still, without the slightest movement of the air. Sunshine, the dazzling glitter of the snow, perfect calm. You would have said it was already spring. From time to time Utkin or I would lay a palm on the leather of Samurai's sheepskin coat. His short coat, dyed black, was hot. Our friend smiled: "Hey, I've got a real solar battery there, haven't I?"

We were through March; it was still fully winter. But we had never felt so intensely aware of the covert presence of spring. It was there. You simply had to know the places where it was hiding while waiting for its time to come.

The cold wind, a little food, and the hot light intoxicated us, plunged us into a blissful drowsiness. . . . But suddenly a gust of wind broke over the cornice of the dune with a sharp hiss and scattered fine snow crystals across our provisions — hunks of buttered bread, hard-boiled eggs. It was time to finish the meal and move on. We put our snowshoes on again and climbed up the white slope, leaving our shelter behind. The icy blast sent long snakes of powder snow to meet us. . . .

At sunset we lapsed into the stillness of the morning. We conversed less and less and were soon completely silent. Out of the bluish mist on the horizon the silhouette of the city was slowly beginning to appear. We were concentrating before the film. . . .

It was in the course of this sixteenth journey that I became aware of an astonishing truth: we were each going to see a different Belmondo! And an hour later, in the darkness of the auditorium, I observed the faces of Utkin and Samurai discreetly. I believed I could understand why Utkin did not join in the audience's uproarious laughter when the gasping writer was struggling up the steep steps of the staircase. And why Samurai's face remained hard and closed when the preposterous publisher was approaching the chained beauty in order to remove one of her breasts . . .

≈ 12 ≈

As we were leaving after the performance we heard a voice in the crowd: "On Saturday they're showing it for the last time. Then that's it. Shall we come on Saturday?"

We stopped dead, all three of us, stunned. The cinema building, the trampled snow, the black sky — suddenly everything seemed as if it had been turned upside down. Speechless, we rushed up to the great billboard, a canvas rectangle four yards by two, showing our hero's face surrounded by women, palm trees, and helicopters. Our eyes locked on the fateful date:

MUST END MARCH 19

When Utkin's grandfather saw our faces, his eyebrows shot up. "What's the matter with you?" he asked. "Have they finally killed off your Belmondo, is that it?"

We did not know what to say. Even in this great hospitable izba where one day the Western World had been born, we felt abandoned.

But life is like that: what we passionately desire often arrives in the guise of what we most dread.

On the day of our final rendezvous with Belmondo, March 19, the day that was going to mark a real end of the world, we saw a new poster! Both different from the previous one and similar, because animated by the brilliant smile and the sparkling eyes that we recognized from a long way off. And the painter must have been perfecting his art — Belmondo looked more alive, more relaxed. This time the shining face was surrounded by animals: gorillas, elephants, tigers. . . .

First there was an explosion of wild joy: It's him, *he* is returning! Then a covert anxiety began to overtake us, a doubt began to gnaw at our fervent hearts: Would he be true to himself? True to us?

Yes, at first this new Belmondo struck us as a brazen impostor, like one of the false czars that Russian history is studded with. Like the false Dmitri or the false Peter III our history teacher had been telling us about . . . Our unease could not be shaken off. That seventeenth showing was to be one of great apprehension.

All through the film we were unconsciously waiting for a gesture from him, a wink. Or a prearranged remark that would have reassured us by testifying to the authenticity of the next film. We focused on him especially in the last scene: now he appears on the balcony, he smiles, he throws down the pages of the typescript. . . . That was where we were hoping for a bridge, a link!

But Belmondo, his left hand resting on the waist of his lovely neighbor, now won over, remained imperturbable. He seemed to be calmly enjoying the suspense, which for us was real torture.

Coming out afterward, we looked again at the poster. Our hero's face, re-created with paint that was too fresh, too vivid, seemed to us artificial. For a long time we stared questioningly at his expression, by the pale light of a nocturnal streetlamp. Its mystery disturbed us. . . .

On the day of the new film we remained silent throughout the journey. Without discussing it, we did not make our usual stopover to eat. Our hearts were not in it. And besides, the weather was not suitable. The frozen fog clung to our faces, stifled our rare words, obliterated the landmarks that guided us. Each of us felt the others to be tense, nervous.

In a little thicket at the edge of the city we took off our snowshoes and hid them, as usual. We did not want to look like villagers. Above all, not in front of Belmondo.

It felt as if we had been waiting a good hour before the lights went down. And as for the newsreel, this time it seemed to last an eternity. We saw a cosmonaut, who looked like a phosphorescent ghost, swimming around his spacecraft with the slow movements of a sleepwalker. We felt we could hear the bottomless silence of space, which surrounded him. But the voice-over, in no way daunted by cosmic hush, announced with vibrant rhetoric: "Today, as all our people and all progressive humanity on the planet prepare to celebrate the one hundred and third birthday of the great Lenin, our cosmonauts, by taking this important step in the exploration of space, offer yet another infallible proof of the universal correctness of the doctrine of Marxism-Leninism. . . ."

The voice went rumbling on in the infinite depths of the cosmos, while the shining phantom attached to the craft prepared to reenter the capsule. He advanced toward the door, which opened inch by inch with appalling slowness, just as if it were sinking into glutinous jelly in a nightmare. It was then that we became aware that we were not the only ones feverishly awaiting the new Belmondo. When the sleepwalking cosmonaut began to thrust his head through the door of the spacecraft and the commentary declared that this excursion into space demonstrated the incontestable superiority of socialism, we heard the furious exclamation of one irritated spectator: "For God's sake! Get on with it! Get back in!"

No, we were not alone in fearing the fraud of a false Belmondo. The whole audience at the Red October cinema was anxious about being betrayed. . . .

From the first moments of the film, everyone forgot these doubts. . . . His muscles stretched to the full, our hero was scaling the wall of a burning apartment building. At every moment, long flames risked setting fire to his black silk cape. And right at the top, on a narrow ledge, the heroine was uttering moans of distress, raising her eyes to heaven, ready to faint. . . .

The hundred and third birthday, the excursion into space of the sleepwalking cosmonaut, the universal correctness of the doctrine — all that was instantly wiped out. The room froze: would he succeed in snatching the swooning beauty from the flames?

This was Belmondo, all right!

When the tension was at its height, when the whole of the Red October was breathing in time with the pace of the intrepid climb, when everyone's fingers were clinging to the armrests of the seats, in imitation of the fingers gripping the ledge on the top story, when Belmondo was hanging on thanks only to the magnetism of our gaze, the incredible occurred. . . .

The camera performed a giddy zigzag, and we saw the apartment building stretched out flat on the floor of a film set. And Belmondo standing up, dusting off his cape . . . A director was haranguing him over some carelessness in his performance. His climb was just a trick! He had been crawling horizontally along a model where the windows were belching forth carefully controlled flames.

So everything was false! But he, he was more real than ever. He had admitted us into the cinema's holy of holies, its very kitchen, and allowed us to see the magic from the other side. So there were no limits to his confidence in us!

What this apartment building laid out on the ground represented was, in fact, the link we had dreamed of, a bit like the spy in the can of fish soup. A link to a world more real than that of the hundred and third birthday and the universal doctrines.

And as initiates into the ways of the West, we now followed Belmondo in his new adventure. Stepping over the windows and walls of the blazing apartment building, he walked out of the film studio.

We rediscovered the West. A world where people lived without worrying about the somber shadows cast by the sunlit mountain-tops. A world of deeds for the sake of the grand gesture. A world where bodies gloried in the power of their own carnal beauty. A world one could take seriously because it was not afraid to show its comic side.

But above all its language! It was a world where anything could be said. Where a word could be found for the most confused, the most murky reality: lover, rival, mistress, desire, affair . . . The amorphous, nameless reality that surrounded us began to structure itself, to classify itself, to reveal its logic. The Western World could read itself!

And, infatuated, we began to spell out the words of this fantastic universe. . . .

This time Belmondo was a stuntman. Though still halfway illit-erate in the language of the West, we nevertheless sensed in this role a powerful, stylish figure. A stuntman! A hero whose courage would always be attributed to someone else. Condemned always to remain in the shadows. To withdraw from the performance at the very moment when the heroine should be rewarding his bravery. Alas! The kiss was placed on the lips of his fortunate double, who had done nothing to deserve it. . . .

In one instance this unrewarding role was particularly harsh. The stuntman had to fall several times from the top of a staircase to dodge a hail of bullets from an automatic rifle. The director, who possessed all the sadistic ways of the publisher in the previous film, made him repeat the exercise relentlessly. Climbing back up again became more and more painful, the fall more agonizing. And each time, a female voice yelled in tragicomic despair: "My God! They've killed him!"

But the hero got up after his terrible fall and announced: "No. I haven't yet smoked my last cigar!"

This line, repeated four or five times, struck a surprising chord in the hearts of the spectators at the Red October cinema. Utkin and I thought at once of Samurai's cigars and those of his former idol in Havana. But the resonance of that exclamation went deeper. The line condensed within it what many of the spectators had been trying to express for a long time. "No, no," a good many of them wanted to say. "I haven't yet . . . " And they could not find the right words to explain that even after ten years in the camps, you could try to make a new start. That even though widowed since the war, you could still have hope. That even in the very depths of Siberia, spring still existed and that this year, make no mistake, there would be a spring bursting with joy and happy encounters.

"No. I haven't yet smoked my last cigar!"

The expression had been found.

And heaven knows how many inhabitants of Nerlug, at the blackest moments of their lives, have since then mentally formulated that response, as they gave themselves a wink of encouragement.

It was after that performance that, for the first time, we spent the night, not with Utkin's grandfather, but in a railroad car. . . .

Samurai took us to the station at Nerlug, and there, striding across the rails, he headed for the farthest of the tracks, half covered with snow. . . . We approached a train standing beside a patch of wasteland. Several trains were asleep in the sidings. Samurai seemed to know what he was looking for. Walking between two freight trains, he suddenly dived under a coach, signaling to us to follow. . . .

We found ourselves in front of a passenger train with dark windows. The city, the sounds and the lights of the station, had vanished. Samurai took a fine steel rod from his pocket and inserted it into the lock. A faint click could be heard, the door opened. . . .

An hour later we were comfortably installed in a compartment. There was no light, but the distant glow of a streetlamp and reflected light from the snow was enough for us. Samurai, who had lit the stove at the end of the corridor, brewed real tea for us — the only real tea there is, the kind they serve on trains on winter evenings. We spread out on the table all the provisions we had not eaten at noon. The scent of the fire and the tea floated into our compartment. The scent of long journeys across the empire . . . Later, stretched out on our berths, we talked about Belmondo for a long time. This time there were no shouts or big gestures. He was too close to us that evening for us to need to imitate him. . . .

That night I dreamed about our hero's new companion. The ravishing stuntwoman. My sleep was transparent, like the snow that had started to fall outside the dark window. I woke frequently and fell asleep again a few moments later. She did not abandon me but settled for a few seconds in the compartment next door. My eyes filled with darkness, I sensed her silent presence behind the thin partition that separated us. I knew I must get up, go out into the corridor and wait for her there. I was sure of meeting her — it was she, the mysterious passenger on the Transsiberian. But each time this dream was ready to take shape, I heard the noise of a train going by on a track next to ours. I had the illusion that it was we who were flying through the night. I fell asleep. And she returned, she was there once more. Our coach hurtled westward. Braving the cold and the snow. Toward the Western World.

So it was not the end of the world. And Nerlug saw two or three more Belmondo films. As if, after a great time lag, these comedies had gone astray, been washed up by the flow of days onto some deserted shore, and waited for long years to come sailing along at last, one after the other.

Belmondo aged slightly, then grew younger again, changed partners, countries, continents, revolvers, degrees of suntan. . . . But that seemed quite natural to us. We believed him to possess a very special kind of immortality, the most inspiring: one that allows you to journey through time — to backtrack or go forward to the brink of decline — only to enjoy the taste of youth more fully.

It was hardly surprising that this time-travel involved so many superb female bodies, so many torrid nights, so much sun and wind.

Belmondo settled in, established his headquarters at the Red October, just halfway between the squat building of the local militia and KGB and the Communard factory, where they manufactured the barbed wire that went to all the camps in that region of Siberia. . . .

He occupied the large billboard, and what people noticed now as they walked along Lenin Avenue was neither the gray uniforms of the militiamen nor the giant skeins of barbed wire being taken away by trucks; it was his smile.

Without admitting it to themselves, the inhabitants of Nerlug were convinced that the authorities had committed an enormous blunder in allowing that man, with that smile, to move in on the avenue. Without being able to explain their intuition, they sensed that this smile was going to play a hell of a trick on the city authorities one day. . . . For already, to their surprise, the filmgoers no longer shuddered at the sight of those gray uniforms, or felt any unease before the horrible trucks with their vile hedgehogs of steel. They saw that smile at the end of Lenin Avenue, next door to the cinema, and they smiled themselves, feeling a boost to their confidence amid the frozen fog.

And on the steps of the liquor store, for the first time in our lives, we witnessed not a brawl but an outburst of laughter. . . . Yes, all those coarse men with ruddy faces were laughing uproariously: they were doubling up, not from the effects of blows smartly delivered to the solar plexus, but from merriment. They banged their thighs with their iron fists, they wiped away their tears, they swore; they laughed! And in their gestures, in their shouts, we recognized the latest Belmondo. He was there among those Siberians, those gold prospectors, those sable hunters, those loggers. . . .

Once again the inhabitants passing the store said to themselves with secret glee: "You know, they were real idiots, those apparatchiks, sticking him up there on the avenue!"

Imperturbable, Belmondo smiled at us from afar.

In our dazzled infatuation we attributed every change to his presence. Everything was closely or distantly linked to him. Like the thunder and lightning at the beginning of April, in the still-wintry sky above the snow-covered city.

We heard a violent storm in the night, as we lay on the berths in our compartment after one performance. A flash froze our astonished faces. The thunder rumbled. We heard it through our dream-stuffed sleep. The motionless train seemed to be hurtling off on a journey in which a marvelous disarray of seasons, climates, and weather reigned. A tropical storm above the kingdom of the snows.

We were eager to go back to sleep, hoping for particularly

sumptuous dreams. But what I saw on that trip turned out to be of an unexpected simplicity. . . .

It was a little station, much more modest than the one at Nerlug, a house lost amid silent pine trees. A waiting room feebly lit by an invisible lamp. The muffled sound of a very few people, they, too, invisible, the stifled yawns of a railroad worker. The smell of a stove where birch logs were burning. And at the center of the room, in front of a timetable that showed only a few lines, a woman. She was attentively examining the arrival times, looking occasionally at the big clock on the wall. In my dream I sensed that for once her wait was not in vain, that someone was definitely coming any minute now. Coming on a strange train whose arrival was not announced on any timetable . . .

The night air, filled with the titillating smell of the storm, penetrated our sleeping coach. It was the freshness of the first breath of air that the traveler inhales as he steps down from the train, at night, in an unknown station where a woman waits for him. . . .

≈ 13 ≈

ONE NIGHT WE STUMBLED onto a brand-new train. . . .

Yes, the coaches had not so far had passengers in them. The green paint was smooth and shining, and the enamel plaques sparkled like white china. The windows, perfectly transparent, seemed to reveal a deeper, more tempting interior. And this interior, with its smell of the virgin imitation leather of the berths, concentrated within itself the very quintessence of train journeys. Their spirit. Their soul. Their voluptuousness.

That evening Samurai did not light the stove. From his knapsack he took out a strange flat bottle and shone a flashlight on it. Then, setting an aluminum cup on the table, he poured himself several drops of a thick, brownish liquid and drank slowly, as if he wanted to appreciate fully its flavor.

"So what's that?" we asked, curious.

"It's a lot better than tea, believe me," he replied, smiling mysteriously. "Do you want a taste?"

"Only if you first say what it is!"

Samurai poured himself some more of the brown liquid and drank it, screwing up his eyes, then announced: "It's liqueur from the Kharg root. You remember? The one Utkin unearthed last summer . . ."

The drink had a flavor we did not manage to identify — or to connect with any dish we had ever tasted. An alcoholic taste that seemed to detach your mouth and your head from the rest of your body. Or rather to fill all the rest with a kind of luminous weightlessness.

"Olga told me," explained Samurai in a voice that was already floating in that aerial lightness. "It's not an aphrodisiac, it's just a euphoriant."

"Afro . . . what?" I asked, baffled by these unfamiliar syllables.

"Eupho . . . how much?" said Utkin, wide-eyed.

The very sound of the unknown words had something volatile and hazy about it. . . .

We lay back on our new berths. Our heads were full of the scene from the film that had most fired our imaginations. It slid imperceptibly into our sleep, which was filled with erotic dreams worthy of the Kharg root. . . .

In this scene Belmondo's ravishing companion, clad in a mere shadow of a brassiere and a trace of a G-string, snatched away a tablecloth, causing a huge vase with a sumptuous bouquet to fall from the table. And with wild abandon she proposed to our hero that they celebrate their carnal communion on this level playing field. The hero evaded the extravagant invitation. And we guessed that it was our own modesty he wanted to protect. The mere appearance of this bacchante was already producing very special vibrations within the walls of the Red October. Belmondo must have sensed that if he had given free rein to his desire, revolution would have been imminent in Nerlug. With the storming of the squat militia building and the destruction of the Communard barbed-wire factory. So he declined the proposition. But so as not to compromise his virility in the eyes of his audience, he suggested quite a different erotic battlefield.

"On the table? And why not standing up in a hammock? Or on skis?"

It is the measure of our love and, indeed, our confidence that this hypothesis was taken totally seriously! Yes, we had cast-iron faith in such a purely Western erotic performance. Two tanned bodies upright (!) in a hammock attached to the velvety trunks of palm trees. The thrust of their desire in direct proportion to the ecstatic unsteadiness beneath their feet. And the passion of their embraces increasing the violence of their rocking. Their fusion, in its profundity, would turn heaven and earth upside down. And those tropical night lovers would come to in the hollow of the hammock, in the cradle of love, whose swinging back and forth would gradually slow. . . .

And as for love on skis, we were well equipped to picture the scene. Who better than we, who spent half our lives on snowshoes, could imagine the intense heat that fired up the body after two or three hours in motion? The lovers would cast aside their poles, the track would grow double, and all that could be heard would be the panting breath, the rhythmic crunching of the snow under the skis, and the cackling of an indiscreet magpie on the branch of a cedar tree. . . .

However, we preferred the hammock, as more exotic. That evening we abandoned ourselves to its rocking, as we floated amid the vapors of the root of love. In our sleep we heard the rustling of the long palm leaves; we inhaled the nocturnal breath of the ocean. From time to time an overripe coconut fell onto the sand, a languorous wave spent itself beside our plaited sandals. And the sky, overloaded with tropical constellations, swayed to the rhythm of our desire. . . .

We woke in the night and lay still for a long moment with our eyes open. None of us dared to confess his amazed intuition to the others. It felt as if the rocking of the hammock were continuing. At first we thought it was a train passing alongside our track and shaking us slightly. . . . Finally Utkin, who was installed on the bottom berth, pressed his forehead against the dark window, trying to penetrate the gloom. And we heard his troubled exclamation: "Hey, where's it taking us?"

Our train was traveling at a brisk pace through the taiga. This was no mere shunting operation on the sidings at the station but speedy and regular progress in good earnest. Not the faintest glimmer of light was visible now: nothing but the impenetrable wall of the taiga and a strip of snow beside the track.

Samurai consulted his watch: it was five to two.

"What if we jumped?" I suggested, gripped by panic but already experiencing the surge of an exciting intoxication.

All three of us went toward the exit. Samurai opened the door. It was as if a frozen pine branch had come and lashed our faces, stopping our breath. It was the last cold of winter, its rearguard action. The needles of the wind and the powder snow. The endless darkness of the taiga . . . Samurai slammed the door.

"To jump out here would be throwing ourselves straight into the wolf's jaws. I bet we've been traveling for at least three hours. And at this speed . . . I know only one man who could do it," he added.

"Who's that?"

Samurai grinned and winked. "Belmondo!"

We laughed. Our fear faded. We went back to our compartment and decided to get off at the first stop, at the first inhabited place. . . . Utkin took out a compass and, after minute adjustments, announced: "We're traveling east!"

We would have preferred the opposite direction. But did we have a choice?

The rocking of the coach quickly got the better of our heroic resistance to sleep. We all dozed off, picturing the same scene: Belmondo opens the coach's door, inspects the frozen night speeding past in a whirlwind of powder snow, and, stepping onto the footboard, hurls himself into the deep shadows of the taiga. . . .

It was the silence and the perfect immobility that woke us. And also the luminous cold of the morning. We grabbed our shapkas and our bags and hurried toward the exit. But outside the door there was no trace of human habitation or of any human activity. Only the wooded flank of a hill, whose white summit was being slowly suffused with the brightness of the rising sun . . .

We remained at the open door, sniffing the air. It was not icy and dry, as at Svetlaya. It entered our lungs with a supple, caressing softness. You did not have to warm it in your mouth before inhaling it, like the harsh mouthfuls of wind at home. The snows stretching out before our eyes made us think of a strange permanent mild spell. And the forest climbing up the flank of the hill was also different from our taiga. In the lines of their branches the trees had a somewhat sinuous delicacy, a little mannered. It was as if they had been drawn in Chinese ink on a background of softened snow, by the hazy light of the rising sun. And around their trunks writhed the long snakes of lianas. It was the jungle, the tropical forest, suddenly frozen in snow. . . .

All at once we saw orange among the trees. . . . Yes, a patch of color like the fragments of bark scattered over the snow between the black trunks and branches. It was Samurai — he was far-sighted — who cried: "Look, it's a tiger!"

And as soon as the word was spoken, the fragments of bark assembled themselves into the body of a powerful cat.

"A Manchurian tiger," breathed Utkin with admiration.

The tiger was there, two hundred yards from the train, and

seemed to be staring at us calmly. It probably crossed the track at this time every morning, and it must have been very surprised to see our spanking-new train upsetting its habits as master of the taiga.

The train moved off, and we thought we could discern the instant tension in the muscles of this royal body, ready to make a long leap to avoid danger. . . .

There was no other stop until the end. We gave up worrying, for we realized that some time back, our journey had turned from a harmless escapade into a real adventure. We must live it as such. Maybe this crazy train would never stop. . . ?

Utkin's compass was now indicating a southerly direction. The sky gradually clouded over, the outlines of the hills became blurred. And the taste of the breeze pouring in at the lowered window escaped all definition: tepid? humid? free? crazy?

Its singular tang became stronger, thicker. And as if the locomotive had finally wearied of struggling against this increasingly dense flux, as if the new coaches were becoming engulfed in this scented stream, the train slowed down, rolled along past some insignificant suburb, then beside a long platform, and finally stopped.

We stepped down from the train into the heart of an unknown city. With the instinct of savages, we followed an avenue that brimmed with the powerful breeze we had already detected in our coach. Now we wanted to reach its source. First came a cluster of ugly low buildings, warehouses with gaping doors, then the dark spires of the cranes. . . .

And suddenly it was the end of the world!

The horizon vanished into soft mist. The land ended a few steps in front of us. The sky began at our feet.

We had stopped on the Pacific shore. It was its powerful breeze that had brought our train to a halt. . . .

We had followed the same legendary route as the cossacks

of old. And, like them, we remained in silence for a long moment, inhaling the iodine scent of the seaweed, trying to grasp the inconceivable.

Now the point of our journey became clear to us. Unable to reach the Western World of our dreams, we had employed cunning. We had headed eastward, to the extreme limit. Yes, all the way to that Far East where the east and the west meet in the misty abyss of the ocean. Unconsciously we had employed the Asiatic trickery of Manchurian tigers: to outwit a hunter following their tracks, they move through the taiga in a great circle, until at a certain moment they are behind their pursuer. . . .

It was thus that, pretending to run away from the unattainable West, we now found ourselves at its back.

We stretched our hands out into the waves lapping below the pebbles. The water had a harsh, salty taste. We laughed, licking our fingers. . . .

Facing the immensity of the ocean, the city seemed almost small. It resembled all the medium-sized cities of the empire. Nerlug, for example: the same rows of prefabricated houses, the same street names — Lenin Avenue, October Square — the same slogans on strips of red calico. But there was also the port and the neighboring district. . . .

It was here that the presence of the West could best be detected. First of all, the ships. With their great white masses, they towered over the bustle on the quays, the mountains of crates, the warehouse buildings. We tilted our heads back to read their names, to admire the fluttering of their many-colored pennants.

The crowd on the streets of the port bore no relation to the gloomy parade of faces that you encountered at Nerlug. The bright coats of the young, smiling women; the black jackets of the sailors, whose lively eyes, wearied by the misty desert wastes of the ocean, hungrily devoured the feast of things and people. From time to time one heard snatches of talk in a foreign language. We would turn. Sometimes we saw the face, with slanting eyes, of a Japanese; sometimes the blond beard of a Scandinavian. It is true that it was quite common to see billboards calling on the people to increase the productivity of their labor or to advance toward the final victory of communism. But here they carried no more weight than that of a splash of color in the panorama of the port district. . . .

Among these women who walked bareheaded, these sailors dressed in short jackets and berets with black ribbons fluttering in the wind; among these foreigners with their light, elegant clothes, we felt like real extraterrestrials. Our sheepskin coats, our great tousled fur shapkas, and our thick felt boots showed that we came from the depths of the Siberian winter. But strangely, we did not feel any unease. We had sensed at once the hospitable character of these streets. They played host to people from the most exotic corners of the globe, people whom nothing could surprise. We walked along in the middle of the animated crowd, breathing in the iodine-scented wind of the mighty deep. . . . And we were no longer ourselves!

We were our dream doubles: Lover, Warrior, Poet.

My gaze, like that of a sparrow hawk, intercepted on the wing the rapid glances of women thrown in our direction. Samurai advanced proudly, a light smile playing on his lips, a glint of tiredness in his eyes — a soldier after a temporary victory in an endless war. As for Utkin, he realized that for the first time nobody noticed the way he walked. For one could not proceed any other way in these streets: the wind threw open the front panels of the women's bright coats, flapped the sailors' broad pants, made foreigners reel. Utkin pointed his shoulder up at the sky, and it was very natural: all the passersby felt as if they were taking off, carried away by the Pacific wind. Furthermore, there was so much to see that we kept stopping all the time. Utkin already knew how to enjoy these pauses, where his limping gait disappeared . . . but in these streets it was pointless to hide it; quite the reverse: his injured foot became the token of a unique personal past in the theatrical melting pot of the crowd.

"It would be good to buy something to eat," the Poet finally dared to suggest.

"All I've got is fourteen kopecks," said the Lover. "A loaf of bread for three, that will be enough."

The Warrior was silent. Then, without explaining anything to us, he headed for one of the human whirlpools in the middle of the little square. We could see people exchanging packages, examining clothes, shoes. A dockside market. Samurai disappeared into the crowd for several minutes, then reappeared, smiling.

"We're going to eat lunch in a restaurant," he announced.

Questions were useless. We knew that Samurai had just sold his "rhinoceros," a gold nugget with a bump reminiscent of the animal's horn — a big nugget, the size of a thumbnail. He had always told us that he would save it for a special occasion. . . .

The waiters looked at us uncertainly, no doubt wondering whether to throw us out or put up with us. Samurai's resolute air and his masterful tone overwhelmed them. They presented us with the menu.

At lunch we talked about Belmondo. Without mentioning his name, we referred to his adventures as if they had been experienced by close acquaintances of ours — or by ourselves. The conversation, somewhere between worldly gossip and a dialogue among secret agents, got under way.

"He was wrong to get himself involved in that business with the theft of the picture," began Samurai in an argumentative tone of voice, as he cut up his steak.

"Yes, especially in Venice!" elaborated Utkin, joining in the game with relish.

"Or at least he ought to have got rid of his mistress first," I added, with assumed indignation. "Because, let's face it, having a girl like that on your hands, stark naked and flaunting her fanny, with a husband as furious as a mad dog . . . for a spy, that's suicidal."

The occupants of the neighboring tables had fallen silent and were turning their heads our way. It was clear that our conversation intrigued them. The three waiters maintained their sullen and scornful expressions. They could not figure out if we were young farmworkers in a fit of delirium or three boy seamen who really had been around the world.

Finally one of them, the one most allergic to fantasies, came over and with a disagreeable grimace muttered: "Okay you kids, pay up quick, and back to school! Everyone's had enough of your idle stories."

We saw several curious smiles spreading over the faces at the neighboring tables. The trio we made was too unusual, even in this restaurant near the docks.

Samurai treated the waiter to a look of mocking indulgence and announced, raising his voice slightly, so as to be heard by everybody: "A little patience. I haven't yet smoked my last cigar!"

And in a leisurely fashion he took out an elegant tube of fine aluminum, from which he removed a real Havana cigar at least eight inches long. With a precise gesture, he cut off a little piece and lit it.

As he blew out the first cloud of aromatic smoke, he said to the petrified waiter: "You have forgotten to bring us an ashtray, young man. . . ."

The effect was sensational. Those at the neighboring tables stubbed out their miserable little cigarettes; the waiters, dumbstruck, vanished into the kitchen. Samurai leaned back in his chair and began to savor his cigar, half closing his eyes, his gaze lost in a far-off dream world. From it Belmondo sent us his warm smile. . . .

That is how we ate Samurai's gold "rhinoceros." He had sold it quickly and therefore cheaply. With the rubles left to him he paid for three third-class seats on a night train. Unreserved seats in a jam-packed coach, piled high with the ill-assorted luggage of travelers who demanded little with regard to comfort, whose humdrum faces and thick clothes were lit by a dim bulb in the ceiling. And that evening's news was broadcast by the radio built into the wall: ". . . in celebration of the seventieth anniversary . . . the Collective has decided to increase by eleven percent . . ."

The locomotive bellowed, and the tonality of its farewell cry gave us a final taste of the Pacific air's misty chill. . . .

The passengers, for their part, uttered a sigh of relief — at last! — and began to take out of their bags provisions wrapped in paper spotted with patches of oil. The carriage was filled with the smell of roast chicken, smoked sausage, melted cheese. Unable to tolerate these alimentary emanations, we climbed all the way up onto the luggage racks. The buzz of all the conversations, muffled by the drumming of the wheels, floated right up to us. It was a non-stop flow, a mixture of everything: alarming anecdotes of legendary delays to this train caused by cataclysmic snowstorms; fears lest their frozen fish might start to melt and drip on their neighbors' coats; hunters' tales; tirades against the Japanese, "who are stripping our taiga bare"; and, of course, inevitable memories of the war, interspersed with the refrain "Mind you, things were better organized under Stalin."

Amid this cacophony, dulled by the thunder from the track, there filtered through clearly the voice of a man of small stature, ageless, a kind of Russified Chinese, whose round face had narrow fissures in it, dark and glistening, out of which his gaze shone. He was sitting in his corner, unremittingly telling stories linked to his life on the banks of the mighty river. His narratives led into one another and formed an epic saga addressed to heaven knows whom. At all events, it was he who proved to be the most resistant to the fatigue of the night. All the other passengers had long since fallen silent, wedged together on the hard benches, trying to find the best position between their neighbors' feet and elbows. But the tale told by the old Chinese was still not at an end. The monotonous and somehow childlike voice of this ageless man filled the darkness. ". . . It was already June, and suddenly the snow began to fall. I had potatoes: they froze. I had carrots: they froze. I had three apple trees: they froze. The river swelled even more. No fish. Then Nikolai said to me: 'In the city, at the game inspectorate, they're giving fifty rubles for every wolf you kill.' And I said to him: 'But first you have to kill it.' And he said: 'Well, those wolves, we're going to plant them.' And I said: 'How d'you mean, plant them?' 'Just like potatoes,' he says to me. And that's what he did. We went into the taiga and found their den. The mother wolf wasn't there. And in the hole, six little cubs. But the inspectorate doesn't give anything for little ones. So Nikolai fixed wire around their paws. And we left them. He said to me: 'That she-wolf will never abandon her young. And the wolves will grow. But they won't be able to walk.' In the autumn we went back. And Nikolai killed them all, with a club, so as not to waste cartridges. I helped him carry them to the cart and then bring them into town. At the inspectorate they gave him three hundred rubles. Nikolai bought eight bottles of vodka, to celebrate. And he drank too much; the doctor said he'd burned his stomach. And then we buried him, and with what was left of the money his wife ordered a good black granite headstone. But the workmen carrying it got drunk and . . ."

I could not bear to hear that voice anymore. I blocked my ears. But the story seemed to seep into my head without words — I could only too easily guess what came next, having heard so much of it. And they got drunk, and the stone fell and broke . . .

Unable to stand it any longer, I toppled down from my narrow plank and began hurrying along the corridor, blocked with luggage and the feet of sleeping passengers. I passed through two coaches similar to our own, filled with the same food smells and the same dull murmur of people crammed in and shaken about, as the passengers in the rear coaches always are. Then there were several second-class coaches, in which the passengers were asleep on berths and obstructing the narrow corridor with their feet, either bare or clad in thick woolen socks. One had to be nimble to avoid them. . . . Finally I came to an empty corridor. The doors to all the compartments were closed. The passengers in this coach were already asleep. . . .

I made my way along three or four more corridors, clean and deserted, redolent of toilet soap. I sensed that the goal of my journey was nigh . . . that mysterious sleeping-car dream car: the one in which a few rare Westerners traveled, venturing into the wild spaces of our fatherland.

I pushed open the door, I sniffed the air, and at that moment I saw her!

She was standing at the window in that narrow space between the long corridor and the platform by the exit doors. She was there, her gaze lost in the darkness of the Siberian night. She was smoking. A slender cigarette, very long and brown in color, which I instantly recognized as the feminine equivalent of Samurai's Havana cigar. A fur cape, light and gleaming, was thrown around her shoulders. Her face, seen in profile by the hazy light of this luxury coach, had nothing dazzling about it. Her delicate features were tinged with the serene pallor of return journeys. . . .

I stopped short a few yards from her, as if I had come up against the invisible aura that her whole person radiated. I feasted my eyes on her . . . that hand holding the cigarette and slightly turning back a lapel of her cape; that foot clad in a short ankle boot, resting on a little ledge against the wall. Her knee beneath the dark transparency of her stocking fascinated me. That delicate knee allowed one to picture a leg that had none of the tanned roundness of the antelopes in our films. No, a slender and vigorous thigh with a fine, golden, velvety skin.

Young savage that I was, I sensed the intimate mystery of this face, this body. In my mind I could never have conceived of it. Nor even have described whom I had encountered. But the savor of her long cigarette and the gleam of her knee were enough for my intuition. As I looked at her, I sensed that her protective aura was slowly dissipating. And it seemed to me less and less impossible that I might hurl myself at this knee, kiss it, bite it, tear the stocking, thrust my unseeing face ever higher. . . .

The nocturnal traveler must have suspected my agony. The ghost of a smile played over her face. She knew her aura was inviolable. To see this young barbarian a couple of steps from her, a savage dressed in a sheepskin and a shapka that smelled of wood smoke and cedar resin, amused her. But where has he come from, this young bear? she must have wondered, smiling. He looks as if he'd like to eat me. . . .

The torture of my contemplation was becoming unbearable. The blood throbbed in my temples, and the words that echoed it were meaningless and yet said it all: "Western Woman! She's a Western Woman! . . . I have seen a real live Western Woman!"

It was then that the train slowed down and began to cross an interminable bridge. It was moving heavily along a track that had become more resonant. Huge steel crosspieces began to march past the window. I rushed to the exit door, I grasped the handle and pushed it violently. The force of the draft and the depth of the black abyss beneath my feet flung me backward.

We were crossing the river Amur.

The breakup that was taking place in its dark immensity was quite different from that symbolic procession of ice blocks that always accompanied the "raising of the revolutionary consciousness of the people" in propaganda films. Symbols like that disgusted us with their tawdry sterility: some aimlessly drifting intellectual contemplating the gutted ice on the river Neva and deciding to commit himself to the Revolution on the spot. . . .

No, the Amur had no interest in contemplative intellectuals. It seemed to be motionless, so slow was its nocturnal gestation. What you saw was an expanse of snow opening up like gigantic eyelids. The black pupil — the water — appeared, expanded, became another sky, a sky upside down. It was a legendary dragon awakening, slowly shedding its old skin, its scales of ice, tearing them from its body. This worn skin, porous, with greenish fissures, formed into folds, broke, hurled fragments against the pillars of the bridge. You could hear the noise of the powerful impact as the current made the walls of the coach vibrate. The dragon uttered a long dull hiss, scraping up against the granite of the pillars, tearing away the smooth snow from the banks with its claws. And the wind carried in the mists of the Pacific — toward which the dragon's head was flowing — and the breath of the icy steppes, where its tail was still lost. . . .

Gradually coming to myself again, I looked at the Western Woman. Her face impressed me with its complete calm. The spectacle, it seemed, amused her. Nothing more. As I observed her, I sensed, almost physically, that her transparent aura was much more impenetrable than I had believed. "It's the breakup on the river Amur," one could read on her lips. Yes, that night was labeled, understood, ready to be recounted.

Whereas I understood nothing! I did not understand where the titanic breathing of the river ended and my own respiration, my own life, began. I did not understand why the light on the knee of an unknown woman was such torture to me and why it tasted the same in my mouth as the mist saturated with marine smells. I did not understand how, knowing nothing about this woman, I could feel so intensely the velvety suppleness of her thighs, imagine their golden softness under my fingers, under my cheek, under my lips. Or why to possess this body hardly mattered once the secret of its golden warmth had been divined. And why spreading this warmth into the wild breath of the night already seemed to me to be an infinitely more vital prize . . .

I understood nothing. But unconsciously, I took delight in it. . . .

The last pillars of the bridge marched by. The Amur vanished into the night. The Transsiberian entered the dense silence of the taiga.

I saw the nocturnal traveler stub out the rest of her cigarette in the ashtray fixed to the wall. . . . Without closing the door, I began to hurry back through the coaches. I knew that I was returning to the East, Asia and the interminable tale of the ageless Chinese. A life where everything was both fortuitous and fated. Where death and pain were accepted with the resignation and the indifference of the grass on the steppes. Where a she-wolf brought food every night to her six little ones whose paws were bound with wire and watched them eat and sometimes uttered a long plaintive howl, as if she guessed that they would be killed and that their absurd deaths would shortly be followed by the death of their assassin, a cruel and absurd one as well. And no one could say why it happened like that, and only the monotonous saga in the depths of a crowded compartment could take account of this absurdity. . . .

I walked along empty corridors and corridors where bare feet or feet in woolen socks stuck out; coaches filled with the heavy breathing and the groans of sleepers; and coaches buzzing with interminable stories of the war, of the camps, of the taiga — all those coaches that separated us from the Western World.

As I climbed onto the narrow plank of the luggage rack, I began to whisper in the darkness for the benefit of Samurai, who was stretched out opposite: "Asia, Samurai, Asia . . ."

A single word says it all. There's nothing we can do about it. Asia holds us with its infinite spaces; with the endlessness of its winters; and with this interminable saga that a Chinese, both Russified and mad — which comes to the same thing — continues to recount in his dark corner. This jam-packed coach is Asia. But I have seen a woman — a woman, Samurai! — at the other end of the train. Beyond the piles of dirty luggage and shopping bags dripping with melting fish; beyond the hundreds of bodies chewing over their wars and their camps. This woman, Samurai, was the Western World that Belmondo revealed to us. But you know, he forgot to tell us that you have to choose that coach once and for all: you cannot be here and there at the same time. The train is long, Samurai. And the Western Woman's coach had already crossed the Amur while we were still getting drunk from its wild winds. . . .

I was tossing these random remarks into the darkness without even knowing if Samurai could hear me. I spoke of the Western Woman, the light on her knee beneath the transparent patina of a stocking, such as we had never seen on the legs of a woman. But the more I spoke of it, the more I sensed the shimmering singularity of my encounter with her slipping away. . . . In the end I fell silent. And it was not Samurai but Utkin (we were lying head-to-foot on our luggage racks) who asked in a nervous whisper: "And us, where are we?"

Samurai's voice answered him, as if emerging from a long nocturnal meditation: "We are the pendulum . . . between the two. Russia is a pendulum."

"In other words, nowhere at all," muttered Utkin. "Neither one thing nor the other . . ."

Samurai sighed in the darkness, as he turned over onto his back, then he murmured: "You know, Duckling, to be neither one thing nor the other is also a destiny. . . ."

I woke with a start. Utkin had nudged me with his foot in his sleep. Samurai was also asleep, with his long arm dangling in space. "Asia . . . the West . . ." So all that had been a dream. Utkin and Samurai knew nothing of my encounter. I derived a strange comfort from this: their Western World remained intact. And in his corner the Chinese was still mumbling: ". . . And this neighbor, when he came back from the war, married another one; he has three big children already; and his first wife, his fiancée, he forgot her long ago. But as for her, she waits for him every evening on the riverbank. She still hopes he will come back. . . . Ever since the war she's been waiting for him . . . waiting for him . . . waiting for him. . . ."

≈ 3 ≈

≋ 14 ≋

THE LAST TIME I went to Paris was in June 1914. . . . My father thought I was big enough to go up the Eiffel Tower. I was eleven. . . ."

That was how on an April evening, in an izba buried amid snowdrifts, Olga began her story.

Once we were back from our trip to the Western World — in other words, the Far East — Samurai had decided that we were ripe for initiation into Olga's secret life. He had revealed its significance to us in brief but solemn tones: "Olga is a noblewoman. And she has seen Paris. . . ."

Taken aback, neither Utkin nor I managed to find words for the tiniest question, despite the crowd of queries buzzing in our heads. The reality of a being who had seen Paris was too much for us. . . .

We listened to Olga. The samovar emitted its light hissing and its soft melodious sighs. The snow tinkled on the windowpane. Olga had swept up her gray hair into a becoming wave, held in place by a little silver comb. She was wearing a long dress edged with black lace, which we had never seen before. Her words were tinged with a dreamy indulgence that seemed to be saying: "I know you regard me as an old madwoman. Well . . . my madness consists in having lived through an era whose richness and beauty you cannot even imagine. My madness is to have seen Paris. . . ."

Listening to her, we learned, with incredulity, of a time when the Western World was practically next door. People went there on vacation! Better still: just to climb up a tower! . . . We could not get over it. So the Western World had not always been a forbidden planet, accessible only obliquely, via the magic of the cinema?

No, in Olga's memories this planet was a kind of picturesque suburb of Saint Petersburg. And from that suburb there had one day come into her family a certain Mademoiselle Verrière, who taught the little Olga a language with strange r's, vibrant and sensual. . . .

"I already understood enough French," Olga confided in us, "to be able to make out the novels my elder sister used to read and which she hid in her bedside cabinet. . . . It was on the train taking us to Paris that I first succeeded in getting my hands on one of these forbidden volumes. One day, when she went out of the compartment, my sister left her book on the berth. I peeped into the corridor: she was busy chatting with Mademoiselle Verrière. I opened the book and immediately came upon a scene that made me forget everyone else's existence as well as my own. . . ."

Olga pours us another cup of tea, then opens a volume with yellowed pages and begins to read softly. . . .

Did she read it in French and give us a translation, a summary? Or was it a text in Russian? I no longer recall. That evening we retained neither the title of the novel nor the author's name. We simply lived amid the dazzling intensity of the images that had abruptly flooded the room in that snowbound izba.

It was a society dinner in a legendary, romantic Paris. A grand supper party after a masked ball . . . The splendor of the decor, the shimmering gold of the candles, the elegant and richly costumed guests at a refined banquet. Sparkling women. Exquisite dishes, decanters, chandeliers, flowers. A young dandy, sitting opposite his mistress, is exchanging passionate glances with her. Suddenly, distracted and clumsy, he drops a fork. He bends down, lifts the tablecloth slightly. . . and the whole world crumbles! His mistress's dainty foot is resting on that of his best friend and gently caressing it. Yes, their legs are entwined, and from time to time they squeeze them together. . . . And when the dandy sits up again, he is greeted by the same loving smile in the eyes of the woman. . . . He flees. He takes flight across the ruins of his love. . . .

Faced with this little feminine foot caressing the perfidious friend's shoe, we were speechless. With those legs intertwined beneath the tablecloth . . . With that fork . . . Nothing in our universe corresponded to the voluptuous subtlety of the scene. We cudgeled our brains to think what foot among our acquaintance could be capable of such a caress and such a betrayal. The images that came to mind were of great felt boots and chapped red hands.

Olga continued reading. The despairing dandy counted on finding some solace with his mistress's best friend. She, at least, should understand and share his pain. And the friend showed herself to be very understanding and compassionate. A sisterly soul seemed to be winging its way toward the unhappy man. . . . But in the midst of his tale of woe the hero noticed that this woman's dress, as she sat before the fire, had slipped — inadvertently, of course — so as to reveal her knee and even the delicate flesh of her thigh. The young man was discreet, thinking that this disarray was due to the emotion his story had inspired. He looked away, hoping that his confidante would finally notice this blemish in her dress. A few moments later he takes another furtive look: the knee and the thigh are exposed to his eyes with what seems an even more flagrant nonchalance. An impossible thought crosses his mind: enticing him with her body, this sisterly soul is inviting him to lose himself between her thighs! The dandy meets her gaze: the woman's eyes are misted over with lust.

So what was there that we could compare with the unimaginable emotional complexity of the Western World that had been revealed to us that evening? In what terms could we express the nuanced eroticism of that seduction scene? The woman sitting in her armchair knowingly baring her leg. A woman continuing to listen to the sorrowful confidences of the young betrayed lover, and showing all the signs of compassion, while at the same time imperceptibly raising the hem of her dress . . . No, we men of the taiga had nothing in our vocabulary to match this sensual dialectic!

Of the three of us, I was the only one who could picture the confidante turned seductress revealing the delicate pink of her thigh. For I had seen her! She was the nocturnal traveler on the evening of our return from the Pacific. It was she. She was also the faithless mistress whose foot caressed that of the perfidious guest beneath the table. I recognized the paleness of her flesh and the elegance of her ankle boot resting on the ledge. "And who knows," I said to myself on the evening of that reading. "If I had not fled like an idiot, maybe the traveler, who turned back the lapel of her cape, might have begun slowly raising the hem of her dress while continuing to stare with exaggerated attention at the dark window!"

So the smile Belmondo was giving us from the end of Lenin Avenue was not so simple. Behind the Western World, seen as a bathing beach for golden antelopes, and the heroic and adventurous West, with its headlong action sequences, lay hidden another one — a voluptuous West, a realm of unimaginable sensual perversions, of refined erotic flourishes, of capricious emotional entanglements. . . .

We paused on the brink of this unknown continent. As our guide we had a little girl from the start of the century, who had one day opened a novel on the Saint Petersburg–Paris train and hit upon these lines that had bewitched her:

> *My mistress had made an assignation with me for that night; gazing at her, I raised my glass slowly to my lips. As I turned to take a plate, my fork fell to the ground. . . .*

All through those days I never stopped thinking about the red-haired woman in her izba buried under the snow. My memory had become even more vivid. Our discovery of the Western World had removed all the tragic sense from that night of the snowstorm: the red-haired prostitute had been transformed, quite logically, into my first amorous adventure, my first conquest. Ardently I awaited the sequel. I could already picture them arriving, my future lovers: sometimes as glamorous spies with robust tanned bodies that promised torrid grappling on the warm ocean beach; sometimes as languorous vamps with decadent and perverse charm. . . .

The red-haired woman provided the substance for these fantasies, the human clay, the bodily lava that I wanted to keep anonymous. All I needed was her physical weight, the heaviness of her breasts, the bulk of her thighs, the warm mass of her hips. This was the material that I sculpted endlessly, impressing onto it the shape of my dreams of the West. It was the amorphous matter waiting to be shaped by the chisel of the Western mind. The breathless chaos of that night of the snowstorm was refashioned as an amorous intrigue; the Redhead's great body was clothed in fine garments and her legs were covered with the transparent patina of stockings. And all that survived of our uneasy coupling beneath a blinding lightbulb was the sensation of an embrace; and this was refined as it segued, via the discreet lighting of a luxury compartment, toward a salon where, sitting in front of the fire, a woman was imperceptibly revealing her delicate nakedness. . . .

Western clarity banished all the untidy elements of that night. The photos spread out on the blanket, her tears, her drunken woman's clumsiness: these now seemed to me like minor blemishes, scraps of clay to be eliminated by the deft and precise chisel.

All this time the red-haired woman was still there in my mind's eye, as it was invaded by female bodies in gestation. And yet she was no longer there: transformed by my cunning craftsmanship, unrecognizable in her new guises. As for her face, I had forgotten her expression since that night. Snow, fatigue, and drunkenness had left it like a washed-out watercolor. This greatly assisted my erotic modeling.

Oddly enough, however, the more the body of the red-haired prostitute became blurred, the more I felt the need to go back to see her, to undergo that first experience again but with quite a new attitude. To obtain a new supply of carnal lava for my fantasies. To possess that great faded body and draw from its primal matter sensations that I would later refine. To make use of its easy abundance, while waiting for the West.

Seeing her again now had a symbolic importance for me as well. I could no longer tolerate the destiny of "neither one thing nor the other." I must make a choice. I could no longer live alternating between that half-mad Chinese, caught up in his interminable saga, and the universe of Belmondo. Between the Orient and the Western World. And the choice made must be final. A visit to the prostitute should draw a line through the saga of Asia. A farewell with no going back.

≈ 15 ≈

It took me a long time to resolve to go to Kazhdai. The days passed, and I was never alone. The six-thirty performance; tea at Olga's: we spent all our free time together.

It was an April evening, mild and silent, that made this farewell encounter possible. . . .

By the afternoon we had all sensed it in the air: winter was about to fight its last rearguard action. The sky misted over, softened, became pregnant with cloudy anticipation. The great flakes began to swirl around in an increasingly powerful, increasingly giddy breeze. It was the start of the final snowstorm. This last gasp, this indolent gale, was winter's way of showing off its power to the victorious spring that was close at hand. Like a great bird, wearied by its seven-month journey, it would flap its great white wings frantically and then would fly away at last, leaving our izbas beneath the soft covering of its snowy quilt. . . .

The next day the village woke up entombed. But this time we sensed that it really was the end of the winter. The layer of snow that I dug into with a wooden shovel had a luminous lightness and caved in on itself, collapsing listlessly. And the sun, up on the surface, was already quite springlike. It shone with warm brilliance on a number of chimneys that rose up out of the snow and on the darkened rooftops. A heavy exhalation emanated from the taiga, the disturbing scent of the mighty reawakening of countless plant lives. And a jackdaw, disproportionately large on a poplar tree that was now quite stunted, called out with mad, abandoned glee. Seeing me emerge from my tunnel, it swung up into the sky, filling the air with its heady cries. Then, in the sun-drenched silence, I heard the murmur of drops forming along the rooftop as it grew warm in the solar rays. The secret birth of the first stream . . .

That evening I headed for Kazhdai. I approached it not from our village but coming from Nerlug. There in the city was where I had just bought something I had never held in my hands before: a bottle of cognac. It was flat and easy to slip into the pocket of my sheepskin coat. I took it out at intervals, turned the cork, which yielded with a pleasant creaking sound, and swallowed a small stinging draft.

All I could see now was the body of the red-haired woman. After each draft I manipulated it more and more deftly, I squeezed it unsparingly. I delved into this flesh to take from it what my dreams would later shape. And I took an increasing pride in my arrogant virility. I saw it as marking the final break with my past. Yes, I must scorn this great amorphous body, humiliate it, impose on it my disdainful strength. And as I slipped across the plain, bathed in coppery light, I thrilled to picture that human clay. My hands were filled with the mass of its breasts, as I pulled and kneaded them, massaging and tormenting their grainy pulp. My hand no longer clung stupidly to her shoulder, as on the first occasion, but plunged into the deep softness of her heavy thighs. I felt I was a sculptor, an artist seeking his raw material in the abundance of a nature that lacked a sense of form. And also a Westerner — a being who focused the proud lucidity of his intellect on his desire, his love, and the female body.

Thanks to Olga's readings, I was daily becoming more familiar with this clarity. I was certain that this marvelous illumination could give an account of our darkest emotions. Even of my visit to the woman I had never loved and whose body frightened me with its weary enormity. My desire to see her again gradually became associated in my mind with the perverse elegance of that woman confidante slowly revealing the soft pink of her thigh. While her eyes retained a light of almost maternal compassion . . .

Yes, at a certain moment I felt I was perverse. And therefore heroic. Liberated from that whole jumble of sentimental trivia my mind had been dragging along in a confused spate. I was perverse, as I understood it, therefore I was a Westerner! And liberated because I was going to have my way with that body — which was all ready and waiting for me — without the least compunction. And I would walk away from it without the red-haired woman knowing that we should never meet again. . . .

Happy to have reached total comprehension at last, I stopped at the summit of a great snow dune that overhung the valley of the Olyei. Screwing up my eyes at the brilliance of the sunset, I turned the cork and drank a long draft of the brownish liquid whose foreign name had such a fine ring to it. And in my head there reverberated these few sentences that in all their Western limpidity expressed perfectly what I was preparing to experience:

> *I know not what desperate impulse drove me to it, but I had, as it were, a subdued desire to possess her one more time, to*

drink all those bitter tears from her magnificent body and then to kill both of us. Ultimately, I both abhorred and worshiped her. . . .

At the station I walked into the main hall with a resolute tread, with the nonchalance of a conqueror. After the Pacific port, everything in this building seemed to me tiny, provincial. The train timetables on the dusty notice board; the dim row of lamps behind their opaque glass bowls; a few travelers with their rustic luggage. I went into the little waiting room. I thought I could already see the glow of her red hair above the rows of chairs. . . . But the woman was not there. Dumbfounded, I made a tour of the main hall: the display case on the newsstand with the faded smiles of the cosmonauts; the buffet with the sleepy attendant; the hoarfrost on the windows. . . . It had not even occurred to me that the red-haired woman might not be there. Especially not on the day of the snowstorm . . . The day of so important and final a choice!

I went out onto the platform. The coaches were asleep under thick eiderdowns of snow. A cleaner armed with a large shovel was slowly opening up a narrow passageway toward the warehouses. "But where can she have got to at this time of day?" I asked myself with irritation, as I contemplated all this provincial stagnation.

Suddenly the very simple answer came into my mind: What a fool I am! She must be with someone. . . . Someone is in the process of "having" her at this moment!

I felt an ill-natured joy stretch my lips into a malicious smile. With swift steps I crossed the station, and using the passageways cut through the midst of the snowdrifts, I headed for the other end of Kazhdai, toward her izba. . . .

"Yes, I'll wait just outside her door," I said to myself. "I'll wait until it's finished. . . ." My perverse desire grew even more intense. On my lips, stimulated by the alcohol, I could detect the taste of her. The Redhead's body would still be hot. A warmed-up mass, ready to be kneaded . . .

All that could be seen of her izba was the top of the roof, the chimney beneath its blackened cap. And the birch tree half buried in the snow, with its little birdhouse. The sun had already disappeared below the castellated line of the taiga. In the April dusk, blue and limpid, the branches of the birch tree, the ridge of the roof, and the contours of the immaculate dunes of snow were outlined with a supernatural distinctness. And in the midst of this serenity I had a strangely detached awareness of my own presence, like a tightly wound spring.

I saw the long dark line in the snow: the passage cut through to the door of her izba. I went up to it, taking care that the crunching of my footsteps should not be heard. The passage was already filled with the violet shadows of the evening.

I saw the steps of packed snow leading right down, toward the door. And leaning over this narrow trench, I peered down into its depths. . . .

To my extreme amazement, the door to the izba was not closed. The steps and the threshold of the house were lit with a soft light. First of all I heard a light knocking, a series of little taps, the sound generally made by a hatchet when you cut small sticks to light the stove. Yes, someone was chopping wood and had opened the door to let some air into the buried izba. This familiar sound disconcerted me. Should I go down straightaway? Or wait a little?

It was at that moment that I heard her voice. . . .

It was a song that seemed to come from very far away, as if it had had to cross infinite spaces before beginning to ripple through this snowbound izba. The voice was almost frail, but it had about it that remarkable freedom, pure and true, of songs sung in solitude, for oneself, for the wind, for the silence of the evening. The words matched the rhythm of the breathing, interrupted from time to time by the crack of split wood. They were not addressed to anyone but melted imperceptibly into the blue shadows of the cooling air, into the smell of the snow, into the sky.

I did not stir as I lent an ear to this voice arising from the depths of the snow.

The tale told by the song was simple. One that any woman might have evoked in the evening, her gaze lost in the fluid dancing of the flames. The despairing wait for a loved one; a bird flying away — happy bird! — over the steppe; frosts that burn the flowers of summer . . .

I knew the story by heart. All I was listening to was the voice. And now I understood nothing anymore!

Here was this voice, simple and soft; the sky whose darkening vastness was filling with the first stars; the pungent exhalation of the nearby taiga. And the solitary birch tree, its birdhouse still empty, this tree keeping an attentive silence in the violet air of dusk.

I stood upright above the passage and looked about me. The song pouring out beneath the sky, rising up from the purple shadows at my feet, seemed to forge a mysterious connection between the limpid silence of the evening and our two presences, so close and so different. And the more I became impregnated with this secret harmony, the more insignificant my febrile fantasies seemed to me. Within my tipsy young head all the arguments advanced in those debates that had obsessed me for so many days were slowly fading. Now came monotonous words, not unlike those of the old Chinese in our coach. Yes, they said, that's how life goes. Here's a red-haired prostitute whose body will quench the desires of young men and old, all of whom will die when their time comes; and another woman will come, brunet or blond, perhaps, and yet other men will seek in her body the elusive spark of love; there will be more winters and more mild spells. And more snowstorms and more summers as short as the instant of pleasure. And there will always be an evening in the life of this woman when she is seated before the fire, softly singing a song that no one will hear. . . .

Thus spoke the impassive voice of Asia in my head.

Another interrupted it, murmuring: The first time, you were naive and unaware; now try to enjoy your desire as you have conceived of it; your understanding of your desire, the triumph of your intellect. Take this body and the range of your sensations, and compose from them a beautiful love story. Tell it, recount it, think it!

The echo of these words fell silent. . . . Moving away from the red-haired woman's izba, I went and sat in the snow, my back against the trunk of a cedar tree. I took off my shapka, I unbuttoned my sheepskin coat. The rippling wind froze my damp brow. A star low in the sky shone like a hesitant tear. This moment in my life had the fragile purity of a tear too. This whole nighttime universe was like a living crystal, suspended on the fluttering eyelashes of an invisible being. I felt I was being watched by that person's immense eyes. I was inside this fragile tear, within its limpid destiny.

The distant voice of the red-haired woman floated up from the narrow passage. That woman with her great faded body, her face eroded by the eyes of all the men who had thrashed around on her belly. That woman who waited endlessly for a train to nowhere, with her carefully trimmed photos and her wine-soaked tears . . .

She was all that. And she was quite different. The voice that soared up toward the trembling of the first star. The white plain overlaid with the blue transparency of the night. The scent of the smoke from the rekindled fire. And those immense eyes that filled the whole vastness of the sky.

My eyelids trembled; everything melted, was troubled. Something warm tickled my cheek as it ran down. . . .

I had never before returned to the village in the middle of the night. I had never spent so long walking on the long ridge of snow above the Olyei, in the shadow of the sleeping taiga. I made slow progress, with no thought of any danger or of the invisible presence of wolves. At moments like this, man is in the hands of destiny, guided by the moonlight like a sleepwalker. . . . I tried hard to remember the red-haired woman's face. In vain. Where I looked for her features there appeared the dim oval painted in watercolors. Suddenly the memory of the photos returned. A young woman holding a child in her arms, her silhouette against the sunlit grass, the glittering of a river . . . As I walked along, I was looking at these smiling eyes.

And like a monogram detected in the middle of tracery, the dull oval lit up, suddenly became clear. The red-haired woman was looking at me with the eyes of the young stranger in the photos. Her face of long ago returned. In my memory of her.

On my return, my aunt said nothing to me. She opened the door, trying not to meet my eyes, and went back to bed, thinking, no doubt, that I was returning from my first erotic rendezvous, my first adventure as a man. . . .

I woke in the middle of the night. As I slept, I thought I had finally understood why the little birdhouse persistently aroused some vague memory in me. It was because it had been constructed with great care and delicacy. The walls, the sloping roof, and the perch were ornamented with fluting carved in wood. It reminded me of the trimmed edges of the photos. These were the vestiges of a hoped-for life that someone had wanted to be beautiful, even in the trivia of existence. "How he must have loved her, that woman!" I whispered softly in the darkness, surprised, myself, by these words.

Several days later, in the blazing sunlight, the village broke loose from its moorings: the Olyei was on the move, shattering its ice, hurtling southward. Toward the river Amur.

Intoxicated by the luminous freshness of this motion, we were overcome with vertigo. The sky turned upside down in the cascading torrent. Our izba's sailed along amid snows still intact, between the somber walls of the taiga.

We were all three of us there, gazing at the slow slide. Utkin stood a couple of steps behind us. It was the first time after all those years that he had come out to see the breakup. . . .

But here the unleashing of the springtime spate had none of the devastating power of the Amur. Nor was there anything symbolic about it. It was quite simply the disintegration of the river's winter shell. A shell of days, memories, moments, taking itself off toward the south amid the melodious creaking of the ice floes and the lapping of the liberated torrents, bombarded by the sun's rays.

As the slabs of ice floated by, we saw the marks of our snowshoes and the holes made by our pikes. Then it was the turn of the Devil's Bend, the deep ruts dug in the snow by the wheels of heavy trucks, and the stippling with black oil. . . .

Suddenly there was an unexpected commotion. A broad section of ice near the little izba bathhouse detached itself, slid down onto the shore, and joined the general convoy. Our eyes were riveted to its angular surface. On it one could see distinctly, molded in the snow, the imprints of two naked bodies. These were the ones left by Samurai and myself on the occasion of our last nocturnal bath, two days previously — the marks of our mute ecstasy as we gazed at the starry sky. These two bodies, with their long legs wide open and their outstretched arms, moved off slowly toward the mighty river. Toward the sun of Asia. Toward the Amur . . .

16

THROUGHOUT THAT DAY of the breakup Utkin remained a little distracted and vague. On account of his painful memory of the river, we supposed. But in the evening, when we were sitting on the first slope to be freed of snow, he drew a crumpled sheet of paper from his pocket and announced with a tense smile: "I want to read you a poem!"

"A poem by Pushkin?" I asked mockingly.

Utkin made no reply, lowered his eyes, and began to read. In an uneven, hoarse voice, which seemed as if it no longer belonged to him. At the first lines I almost let out a whistle. Samurai swiftly stopped me with a cold look.

"I know your vigil underneath this snow
Is more despairing far than death. . . .
I know if I came close to you
I'd simply earn a pitying glance.
But I will not approach.
I'll stay here in the plain's cold fog
To be a presence in white emptiness,
A distant figure. So that you can dream
Of him who comes eternally to meet you
But never arrives. . . ."

At the last words, Utkin's voice became choked. He thrust the paper into the pocket of his sheepskin coat, got up abruptly, and began running along beside the Olyei, sinking into the soft snow. He looked more than ever like a wounded bird attempting to fly. . . .

We were silent. Samurai took out his cigar and lit it with a slow gesture. He looked pensive. Exhaling the bitter smoke, he raised his eyebrows, gently shaking his head to the rhythm of his silent thoughts. Then, noticing that I was watching the course of his reflections on his face, he clicked his tongue and uttered a sigh.

"You know, women are stupid. For a poem like that they should risk perdition! But they like handsome little guys like you or great hefty ones like me. Look at him . . . he's running along like a madman. There. He's fallen down, poor fellow! . . . No, no. We should leave him alone right now. . . ."

Samurai fell silent. In the distance we saw Utkin get up, shake off the snow stuck to his sheepskin, and continue his limping progress toward the first trees of the taiga. . . . Suddenly Samurai smiled and gave me a wink.

"Admit it. He would never have had the courage to read us his poem if we hadn't seen Belmondo! Maybe he wouldn't even have written it. . . ."

We returned to the village by the fluid blue light of the springtime dusk.

"Go and knock on his door," Samurai instructed me. "Tell him they're showing the film for the last time tomorrow. Who knows when we'll ever be able to see it again. Either this one or any others. Maybe not before next winter . . ."

Next day at six-thirty, after the achievements of socialist labor and the distribution of decorations at the Kremlin, we entered a fairy city that arose from the depths of the sea. Venice! And the indomitable Belmondo was racing along at the wheel of a speedboat, cutting himself a path between languid gondolas. In flight from his pursuers, he and his ship of fools hurtled straight into the lobby of a luxury hotel, whose first floor was scarcely higher than the level of the canal. The glass doors were smashed to smithereens, the staff took cover in protected corners. And smiling indulgently, he announced with a grand gesture: "I have reserved the royal suite for tonight."

How many lips there were in the heart of our taiga that spring murmuring the magic word *"Venetsia!"*

Samurai had got it right: after that showing Belmondo took a vacation. As if, now that it was summer, his presence at the end of Lenin Avenue was less indispensable. And it is true that as the trees cloaked themselves in the verdant shadow of the first leaves, they gradually hid the squat building of the militia and the KGB, and softened the angular contours of the barbed-wire factory.

But more than anything, that West which he had sought to acclimatize on the permafrost of our lands seemed to be taking root. The summer will take care of the rest, he must have thought, as he went off on vacation.

Yes, the Western World now seemed firmly grafted into our hearts. Was it by chance that even the stupid newsreels, showing the gold armor plating of those Kremlin medals and the Stakhanovite weavers, now inspired a kind of tremor in our breasts? We remembered that back in the winter those weavers and those bemedaled old men used to precede the appearance of our hero. Now they were almost dear to us. And to our amazement, it was behind the masks of these propaganda robots that we discovered the first nostalgia of our lives: nostalgia for those long journeys through the snow-covered taiga, the complex constellations of scents, luminous tones, and sensations. . . .

One summer's evening all three of us were gathered around Olga's samovar, listening to her tale. She was telling us about a writer whose novel she could not read to us, first of all because the book was too long — it would take years to read, she said, and a whole lifetime to understand — but also because it was evidently not translated into Russian. . . . She therefore confined herself to summarizing a single episode, which, she claimed, expressed the idea of it. . . . The hero was, like us, drinking tea, although he did not enjoy the benefits of a samovar. One perfumed sip and a mouthful of a cake with an unknown name produced a miraculous reaction from his taste buds: in him were reborn the sounds, the smells, and the spirit of the distant days of his childhood. Without daring to interrupt Olga's story, or to admit this insight, we asked ourselves, astonished, incredulous: "What if an image seen scores of times — that of the weaver; or the cool smell of shapkas covered in melted snow; or the darkness of the auditorium at the Red October — what if all those could take the place of the young French aesthete's cake? What if we, too, could have access to this mysterious Western nostalgia, with the rudimentary means we have at hand?"

With Belmondo, one miracle more or less was not a problem. . . .

But it was the language of the West, even more than the themes of its novels, that was taking root in us.

For us the German that we learned at school had no link with the Western World of our dreams; it was the language of the enemy, a useful instrument in case of war: that is all it was. The language of the Americans was repugnant to us. The children of the local Party elite mouthed it to a greater or lesser extent. They were all even put into a special group created for students of English. Proletarians, on the other hand, had to learn the language of the enemy. . . .

No, for us the only real language of the Western World was Belmondo's. Seeing his films ten, fifteen, twenty times over, we learned to make out on his lips the inaudible traces of those phantom words eliminated by the dubbing. A little trembling at the corners of his mouth when the sentence in Russian was already completed, a swift rounding of his lips, stresses that we guessed were even . . .

Sometimes Olga read to us in French. Little by little the phantom phrases showed through. Belmondo was beginning to speak to us in his mother tongue. Our desire to respond to him was such that French seeped into us by impregnation, without grammar or explanation. We copied its sounds, like parrots at first, then like children. Besides, thanks to the films, we had been speaking it before we ever heard it. Our lips, imitating the movements observed on Belmondo's, repeated, all unaided, the lines that Olga read out before the open window in the clear soft evening:

"Impossible union
Of souls through the body . . ."

In these verses of a poet of long ago all our youthful dreams found vivid expression. . . .

One day Utkin spoke to Olga about English. She gave him an aristocratic smile, the corners of her mouth a little tensed: "English, my dear friends, is nothing other than bastardized French. If I remember correctly, until the seventeenth century French was the official language of the English. As for the Americans, let us not speak of them. They contrive to express the few ideas they have left entirely through the most basic interjections."

Her exegesis delighted us. So in their ignorance, what the little apparatchiks were studying was a vile surrogate for Belmondo's language! And it was, furthermore, entirely replaceable by a series of primitive gestures and interjections. Utkin was the one who derived the greatest satisfaction from this explanation. The Americans were his pet hate. He could not forgive them for the extermination of the Indians. In his perception the North American Indians were none other than our distant Siberian ancestors who had long ago crossed the Bering Strait and settled all over the great prairies of America. "They are our very close brothers," he would often say. He envisaged a military alliance with the Indians against the Americans. And when the fighting was over, New York must be razed to the ground and the lands annexed by the whites returned to the bison and the Indians. . . .

Belmondo departed. The great portrait of him beside the Red October cinema disappeared, making way for various glum faces from a film about the civil war. But the West was still there among us. We sensed its presence in the spring air; in the transparency of the wind, in which we sometimes detected the piquant tang of the ocean; in people's relaxed expressions.

And while the three of us, in love with the West, sought out its secret essence in books and in the music of its language, there were other devotees, who discovered it in more tangible portents. The stunning coup de théâtre pulled off by the school headmistress, for example.

This was the woman who, according to rumors as persistent as they were improbable, indulged in sexual orgies on narrow berths in the cabins of the big trucks that transported vast cargoes of timber. A woman who was forever muffled up in a shawl; who wore a jacket and a skirt of very thick wool, as stiff and as solid as that used for carpets; her feet shod in great fur boots that revealed only a couple of inches of her calves, which were further protected by knitted leggings. A woman, in a word, whose body was inaccessible, unimaginable, nonexistent. And whose face was the face of a faded woman, reminiscent of a padlocked door that no one would ever have wanted to open in any case . . . And, suddenly, *this* coup de théâtre!

On that day in May we saw an extraordinary car pull up in an alleyway that ran beside the school building in Nerlug. A foreign make such as we would come across only in films about the horrors of capitalism in its death throes. And in those of Belmondo, of course . . . We already knew that by means of astute bartering it was possible to get yourself one of these cars in the Far East from the Japanese. But it was the first time we had seen one "in the flesh."

It was certainly not new. It must have been sprayed and resprayed, repaired several times, tampered with, perhaps. Its license plate looked like that of any old truck. But what did we care? What counted was its noble profile, its streamlined silhouette, its unfamiliarity. In a word, its Western air.

It all happened very quickly. The passersby and we students did not even have time to crowd around the beautiful stranger. Its door slammed; and a tall, well-built man, wearing the uniform of an officer in the merchant marine, emerged and took a few steps, while keeping his eye on the school gate. Everyone followed his gaze.

A woman came down the flight of steps. The headmistress! Yes, it was she. . . . We instantly forgot about the car. For the woman who walked over to the captain was very beautiful. We saw her legs revealed up to the knee, long, svelte, the light shining off her black stockings. We could even see her knees, which were elongated, elegant and delicate. And furthermore she had breasts and hips. Her breasts were slightly uplifted by the fine lace that framed the very modest décolletage of her dress. Her hips filled the fine material with their rhythmic movement. She was quite simply a beautiful woman, confident in her gestures, smiling as she went to meet the man waiting for her. Her swept-up hair revealed the pretty curve of her neck; on her ears sparkled pendants decorated with amber. And her face, in its fresh and open candor, was like a bouquet of wildflowers.

At the moment of their meeting, of course, all we saw was this bouquet. The other features of the transfigured headmistress were imprinted in our eyes but examined only later, with the aid of our collective memory. The coup de théâtre was too rapid.

She crossed the spring street. The captain took several steps toward her, with a somewhat mysterious smile hovering on his face. Then, with the flourish of a conjurer, he removed his fine blue nautical cap and bowed to the woman who stood in front of him. The crowd held its breath. . . . The captain kissed the headmistress on the cheek. . . .

So they did know how to do all that! She to dress elegantly, groom her hair, be lively, desirable; he to master that handsome machine, open the door for a lady with a courteous remark. And, above all, to take off Belmondo style!

Yes, he did it for us, driving through the red light, defying the gray uniforms, chewing up the streets of Nerlug with his four fearsome wheels. The roar of the beautiful stranger deafened us; its speed distorted all normal perspectives — trees and houses seemed to be hurtling toward us. And the car, with squealing tires, was already turning into Lenin Avenue. At the open window we saw a flash of our headmistress's pink scarf fluttering in the wind. Like a gesture of farewell.

A week later the city discovered the key to the mystery. . . . On the day of the last snowstorm the headmistress had decided to go and see this film, at the very first showing of the day. So as to be sure of not being surprised there by her pupils. Everyone had been talking about this Belmondo for months. But she had not cared to stoop to that type of mass culture. However, the temptation was great. The headmistress must have sensed a wind of change blowing in the streets of Nerlug. . . .

The day after the storm, hardly had the snowplows cleared the principal thoroughfares of the city than she went to the cinema. Armored in her carapace of thick wool, she noted with satisfaction that she was practically alone in the auditorium. . . .

The captain arrived only after the newsreel. A disciplined man, he found his row and his seat and sat down beside her. He wore the expression he had on bad days — days when he needed to leave the ship and plunge into the bustle of everyday life, become a man like other men. He was on his way to Novosibirsk: his train had been blocked at Nerlug by winter's rearguard action; its departure was not forecast for another twenty-four hours. Exasperated by the futile wait, badly shaved, peevish, the captain ended up in the cold auditorium of the Red October cinema, next to a woman of whom he thought, with disgust: So this is a woman of Nerlug. . . . Heavens above! How can a woman get herself up like this? My sailors could do better. A pretty face, but that expression! She looks like a nun in the middle of Lent. . . .

The lights went out. Colors filled the screen. A legendary city arose from the azure sea. With its palaces, and its towers reflected in the water . . . And the captain immediately forgot Nerlug and his train and the Red October; and as he recognized the silhouette from the air, he murmured: *"Venetsia."*

The headmistress's long lashes trembled. . . .

Belmondo arose, concentrating within his gaze all the magnificence of the sky, the sea, and the city, and sped off along the canals in his crazy boat.

"I have reserved the royal suite for tonight," he declared, crash-landing in the hotel lobby at the wheel of his launch.

A gentle echo vibrated in the hearts of the two solitary spectators: "The royal suite . . . For tonight . . ."

And in the suite in question a kind of bacchante, on stiletto heels and wearing very little else, snatched off the tablecloth and invited the hero to a wild orgy: "You're going to have me on this table right now."

The headmistress stiffened, feeling the hairs on her temples grow tense. The captain coughed.

"And why not standing up in a hammock? Or on skis?" retorted Belmondo.

It was too silly for words! Wonderfully silly! Astounding! The captain began to laugh heartily. The headmistress, no longer able to resist the laughter welling up, did the same, pressing a lace-edged handkerchief to her lips. . . .

And once again the city could be seen rising out of the waters of the lagoon, but this time arrayed in its nocturnal beauty. Belmondo appeared, caught in that fleeting moment of a tremor of the soul between two adventures. He was sitting on a granite parapet, with a muted look and a melancholy air. We had always taken these moments to be a necessary pause between the action sequences. But two solitary spectators read quite a different meaning into this silent parenthesis. . . . It was then that the captain, turning his head slightly toward his neighbor, repeated dreamily: *"Venetsia."*

As for the rest of us, gawking onlookers fascinated by the Western machine on that day in May, the extent of the upheaval provoked in our lives by Belmondo was clearly borne in on us. If a car newly emerged from one of his films could rip up the frozen perspective of Lenin Avenue and transform our headmistress into a creature of fantasy, something had changed forever. The gray uniforms, we knew, would invade the streets again; the Communard barbed-wire factory would increase its productivity and exceed the plan; winter would return. . . . But nothing would be as it was before. From now on our lives would open out into an infinite elsewhere. The sun, trapped among the watchtowers of the camp, would gradually resume its majestic pendulum swing back and forth.

Nothing would ever be as it had been before. Oh, how we longed to believe this!

≈ 17 ≈

WHEN DID IT finally happen?

That young female body taking me, shaping me, inhaling me, absorbing me into its scents, into the ephemeral suppleness of its skin, into the dark smoke of its hair spread out upon the grass. With the strong, warm wind of early summer blowing, the wind from the steppe — such a contrast with the ice-cold torrent of the Olyei, whose crystalline waters in spate surrounded us on all sides. And the hammock swaying in the wind . . . Yes, a hammock! We had forgotten nothing, Belmondo! That wind. The sky overturned in her slanting eyes, blinded with pleasure, her breathless moaning . . . When was it?

Belmondo's arrival had interrupted the regular passage of time.

Winter no longer implied endless sleep. Nor the evenings — because of the films — quietude at the end of the day. The hour of six-thirty had imposed itself on everyone with apparent universality. We lived subject to these new rhythms, finding ourselves in Mexico one day, in Venice the next. Any other concept of time was obsolete. . . .

It is impossible for me to remember now whether it was Year One or Year Two of our new chronology. Impossible to say whether I was fifteen, as in that spring when we absconded to the Far East; or sixteen — that is, a year after Belmondo's arrival. I simply do not know. In all probability, however, it was the second spring. For I could not have lived through all that I did in a single year. My heart would have exploded!

Fifteen, sixteen . . . These methods of reckoning are in any case so relative, given the vibrant intensity of our passions. Here is what I lived through: the age of the night in the red-haired woman's izba; the age of my first mouthful of cognac; the age of the salt taste of the Pacific. The age when I discovered that the fragile beauty of a woman's knee could cause devastating pain, could be blissful torture. The age when the soft white flesh of an aging prostitute haunted me with its insurmountable physicality. The age of the unveiled mystery of the Transsiberian. The age when a woman's body taught me its language, word by word, gesture by gesture. The age when childhood had become no more than a faint echo — like the memory of that great frozen tear in the eye of the wolf stretched out full length on the blue-tinted snow of the evening.

Fifteen, sixteen . . . Here is what I was. A strange alloy of the winds, silences, and sounds of the taiga, of places visited or imagined. Someone who already knew, thanks to Olga's library, that feudal chatelaines had long bodices, like the bodice of the unhappy Emma Bovary. That the shoulders of a bathing odalisque were tinged with amber . . . And that only a real boor, like that country squire in Maupassant, would ask a hotel manager to prepare the bed at midday, thus revealing his intentions with regard to his crimson-faced young wife . . . Having studied Musset, I knew that romantic lovers always choose a cold, sunny morning in December to part forever — the clarity of past passions now spent, the vivid bitterness of feelings now subdued. I was somebody who observed the monstrous decomposition of the flesh of Zola's Nana, shaking my head in violent denial: No, no, beyond this human clay doomed to disintegration, there is something else! There is that song that arose from the depths of the snow and poured out into the dark-purple April sky. . . . And in that hotel bedroom at the Golden Lion I was to perceive something that many readers in the West had not even noticed: on the mantelpiece, glimpsed in a brief phrase, there were two big seashells. You had only to hold them to your ear — had Emma done it? I often wondered — and you could hear the faint roar of the sea. With our mad dreams of the Pacific, how close we felt at such moments to that adulterous woman!

Belmondo gave to the alloy that I was a structure, a movement, a personified outline. With all his joyful strength he brought our present and our dreams closer together. I was at an age when this fusion still seemed possible. . . .

So it must have been at the start of summer. An evening filled with a blue wind from the steppes. On an island in the middle of the river in spate — a narrow grassy strip with a ruined izba and the remnants of an orchard, several apple trees foaming with white blossom.

In the distance, in the golden haze of the sunset, rose the taiga, its feet in the river, reflected in the somber mirrors of the water that now reached into its shady recesses.

The little island floated in the glow of the evening. The noisy rippling of the current mingled with the rustle of the wind in the blossoming branches. The cool little waves lapped insistently, breaking against the sides of the old boat I had moored to the rail of the flooded izba steps. The day was slowly fading, the light was turning mauve, lilac, then violet. The darkness seemed to refine the living harmony of the sounds. We could hear the slight scraping of the boat against the wood of the steps now, the serene cry of a bird, the silky whispering of the grass.

We were stretched out at the feet of the apple trees, lying against each other, our eyes wandering amid the first stars. Naked, she and I, the warm wind enveloping our bodies with its breeze steeped in the aromas of the steppe. And above our heads, fastened to the great stunted branches, a hammock swung gently in the wind. Yes, we had remained true to Belmondo, down to the smallest details of the setting for our love scene. We had climbed into that unstable craft and tried to stand up, embracing each other and quickly losing our heads. . . . But either our desire was too violent or the erotic savoir faire of the West still escaped us. . . .

We found ourselves in the grass, scattered with white petals: we hardly noticed our fall. We felt we were still falling, still flying, still loving each other in flight. . . .

Her supple body slipped away, escaping in our fall through the air. I did not succeed in holding onto it. With my frenzied heaving I was pushing it along on the smooth grass toward our island's ephemeral frontier at the water's edge. I had to wrap the cascade of her hair around my fist. As the cossacks used to do in the old days, lying on bearskins in their yurts. My desire had a memory of that gesture. . . .

She was Nivkh, a native of the forest of the Far East where we had once seen a tiger, blazing in the snow. . . . Her face was framed with long, glossy black hair; she had slanting eyes, the enigmatic smile of a Buddha. Her body had skin that seemed to be covered with a golden varnish and the reflexes of a liana. When she sensed that I would not let her go, her body twined around me, molded me, absorbed me through all its trembling vessels. She permeated me with her scent, her breath, her blood. . . . And I could no longer make out where her body merged into the grass filled with the wind from the steppes; where the savor of her round, firm breasts mingled with that of the apple blossom; where the sky of her dazzled eyes ended and the somber depths glistening with stars began.

Her blood flowed in my veins. Her breathing filled my lungs. Her body writhed into me. When I kissed her breast I was drinking the foam from the snowy clusters in the orchard. I thrust myself into that nocturnal space through which the wind had traveled, perfuming itself with a thousand aromas, carrying away with it the pollen of countless flowers. She cried out as she sensed the peak approaching, her nails tore at my shoulders. A crazy liana intoxicated with the sap of the trunk it held entwined. I flooded her, I filled her with myself. In her I touched the giddy depths of the sky, the cool of the dark waves. Her heart was already beating somewhere beyond the nocturnal taiga. . . .

The wind scattered white petals over our bodies as we lay there in the blissful exhaustion of love. The wood fire we had lit on arrival flared up at intervals into a tall red plume, then quieted down, stretched out on the ground in the silent glowing of its embers. The boat fastened to the steps of the izba, washed occasionally by a wave, gave out a whisper, followed by sleepy lapping. And the hammock, the hammock of our crazy fantasies, swung about our heads amid the bubbling foam of the blossom. It looked like a fantastic net hurled into the dark heavens by a demented fisherman so as to make a catch of quivering stars. . . .

On a gray, calm day in July that same summer I was walking in the streets of Nerlug, a bag of provisions in my hand. The gardens were spilling their abundant foliage over the fences. In the courtyards you could hear the lazy clucking of hens. The sparrows bathed in the warm dust at the sides of the little streets. Everything was so familiar, so ordinary! There was just me, carrying within me, through this tranquil day, the trembling immensity of my first love.

I was waiting in line with several women in front of the ticket window in the little building at the bus station. Filled with my secret fever, I did not at first pay any attention to their talk. Suddenly the name of the Redhead broke in on my blissful oblivion.

"But what could he do? They fished her out a good three miles below the bridge. Doctor or not, what do you expect him to do?"

"I don't know. . . . Artificial respiration, maybe. They say that helps."

"Well, she was completely rotten already, that one, I tell you. And if it wasn't that, it would have been syphilis or some such. . . ."

"She had it coming to her. When I think of the number of folk she passed on her filth to . . ."

That last observation seemed to the women too harsh. They fell silent, lowering their eyes and turning away, but internally they must have approved of the remark. It was then that an old woman with fine, pale lips, who had so far said nothing, began to talk, giving little chuckles as if to relax the atmosphere: "I've seen her. Hee, hee, hee! I've often seen her at the train station, that one! She was real crafty, I can tell you. More than most. All the time she pretended she was waiting for a train. She went this way, she went that way. She looked at the clock. As if she was a passenger. Hee, hee, hee!"

"Some passenger! A filthy cow!" cut in one woman, adjusting the straps on her knapsack. "May God forgive me, but I tell you she had it coming to her!"

I left my place in the waiting line and pushed open the door. As I came away, the sound of that little laugh grated in my head like ground glass. . . . I went to Kazhdai.

I did not have the courage to go right up to her izba. I saw the door barricaded with two long crossed planks, the window with its panes broken. The branches of the birch tree held hidden within their foliage the light, tuneful lives of several invisible birds. A pure and delicate song in this silent garden . . .

I left, taking the same route as in winter. But at this season the plain that led down to the Olyei was all covered with flowers.

The death of the red-haired woman — or rather the conversation about her suicide — decided me: I must go away. Leave the village, escape from Nerlug, never again set eyes on that country where ultimately the saga of the old Chinese would triumph over the elegance of the Western World and its adventures. Where in some dark corner of a bus station you would hear the grating of ground glass. And once Belmondo had gone again, this grating and grinding would crop up all over the place. It would be the sound of the heavy boots of prisoners taken out in serried ranks to do hard labor; the strident screaming of the saws biting into the tender flesh of the cedar trees; and the clatter of the coupling between the coaches on the Transsiberian — which no one would wait for in Kazhdai anymore. This grinding would once more become the very stuff of the harsh life of all who lived here. Of those, in fact, who did not know how to escape it by fleeing west of Lake Baikal, west of the Urals, beyond that frontier, invisible but so substantial, with Europe.

Yes, I had decided to flee as quickly as possible. I wanted to tear myself away from the liana that penetrated further into my body every night. Flee my love. My mute love. My beautiful Nivkh upturned onto me the starry sky that flashed in her slanting eyes, she drew me in a giddy tumble through the wind of the steppes. Her love mingled our cries with the bellowing of the stags in the moonlit forest skirts; our bodies with the wild flow of the resin on the cedar trunks; the beating of our hearts with the throbbing of the stars. But . . .

But this love was mute. It did without words. It was impenetrable to thought. And I had already had my European education. I had already tasted the terrible Western temptation of the word. "What is not said does not exist!" this tempting voice whispered to me. And what could I say about my Nivkh's face with its Buddha's smile? How could I focus my mind on that fusion of our desire with the mighty respiration of the taiga and the waves on the Olyei without carving everything up into words? And killing the living harmony?

I aspired to a love story. Told with all the complexity of Western novels. I dreamed of breathless confessions, love letters, seduction strategies, pangs of jealousy, intrigue. I dreamed of "words of love." I dreamed of words. . . .

And one day when we were walking in the taiga, my Nivkh suddenly went down on her knees and carefully parted the tangle of leaves and the tufted layer of moss. I saw a plump brown bulb, from which grew, balanced on a short, pale stem, a flower of an unspeakable delicacy and beauty. Its oblong body, transparent mauve, seemed to be gently quivering in the half shadow of the undergrowth. And as always, Nivkh said nothing. Her hands thrust into the moss seemed to be faintly illumined by the calyx of the flower. . . .

I had made up my mind. And as the intensity of our longings logically gives rise to coincidences that do not occur at normal times, I soon received apparent encouragement. . . .

When I got back from Kazhdai I took a crumpled newspaper out of my shopping bag. It was a rare newspaper, impossible to find even on the newsstands of Nerlug. One of the papers we were always so pleased to pick up off the seat of a bus or in a station waiting room. A *Leningrad Evening News,* left behind, no doubt, by some traveler whom a bizarre chance had brought to our doomed territories.

I read all four pages straight through, leaving out neither the Leningrad television programs nor the weather reports. It was odd to learn that two weeks previously, in that fabulously distant city, it had rained and the wind had blown from the northeast. It was on the fourth page, between the help wanted and the advertisements for the sale of pets (poodle puppy, Siamese cats . . .), that my eye lit upon these few lines surrounded by a decorative border:

THE LENINGRAD COLLEGE
OF CINEMA TECHNICIANS IS
OPENING ITS RECRUITMENT OF
STUDENTS FOR THE FOLLOWING
SPECIALTIES: ELECTRICIAN,
EDITOR, SOUND ENGINEER,
CAMERAMAN. . . .

My aunt came back into the room. With a rapid gesture, I hid the newspaper, as if she could have guessed the grand project that was setting me alight. It was no longer a simple desire to escape but a precise objective. Leningrad, a misty city at the other end of the world, was becoming a great step in the direction of Belmondo. A springboard that would project me — I was sure of it — into a meeting with him.

Toward the end of the month of August, on a very bright evening, which already smelled of autumnal freshness, my aunt called me into the kitchen in a voice that struck me as strange. She was sitting, very upright, at the table, wearing a dress she put on only for holidays, when her friends were coming. Her big hands, with their firm, bony fingers, were absently rubbing the corner of the tablecloth. She was silent.

Finally, taking the plunge, she spoke without looking at me: "It's like this, Mitya. I must tell you. . . . Verbin and I, we have thought about this for a long time and . . . and we're going to get married next week. We're old, it will make people laugh, maybe. But that's the way it is. . . ."

Her voice broke off. She coughed, put her hand to her mouth, and added: "Wait a moment. He should be coming. He wanted to meet you. . . ."

But we know each other very well! I was on the point of exclaiming. But I held my peace, realizing that it was more a question of a ritual than of a simple introduction. . . .

The ferryman appeared almost at once. He must have been waiting in the courtyard. He had put on a light-colored shirt, with a collar that was very wide for his wrinkled neck. He came in with an awkward gait and gave me an embarrassed smile as he held out his only hand to me. I shook it with a lot of warmth. I really wanted to say something encouraging, something friendly, to them, but the words would not come. Verbin, still with his awkward gait, went up to my aunt and placed himself beside her, as if standing to attention rather indecisively.

"There you are," he said, moving his arm slightly, as if to say: What's done is done.

And when I saw them like that, one next to the other, those two lives so different but so close in their long and calm suffering, when I recognized on their simple and anxious faces the outward show of that timid tenderness that had brought them together, I ran out of the room. I felt a salt lump constricting my throat. I went down the steps outside our izba, removed the plank at the bottom, which was overgrown with wild plants, and took out a tin box. I went back into the room, and before the amazed eyes of my aunt and Verbin, I emptied out the contents of the box. The gold shone. Some sand, some tiny nuggets, and even some small yellow pebbles. All that I had accumulated over the years. Without a word, I turned and fled outside.

I walked along beside the Olyei; then, when I came to the ferry, I sat down on the thick planks of the raft. . . .

What had just happened only convinced me more: I had to leave. These people, who were, I now understood, so dear to me, had their own destiny. The destiny of that enormous empire that had crushed them, mutilated them, bruised them. Only at the end of their lives were they managing to make a new start. They had come to realize that the war was well and truly over. That their memories no longer interested anyone. That the snow crystals that landed on the sleeves of their sheepskin coats still had the same sparkling delicacy. That the spring wind still brought the perfumed exhalation of the steppes . . . And at that very moment they had seen a remarkable, radiant smile appearing at the end of Lenin Avenue. A smile that seemed to warm the frozen air within a radius of a hundred yards. And they felt this breath of warmth. In the spring they rediscovered the veiled beauty of the first leaves. They learned to hear again the rustling of those transparent canopies, to notice the flowers, to breathe. Their destiny, like an enormous wound, was healing at last. . . .

But I had no place in this life of convalescence. I had to leave.

18

THE DAY I LEFT, in September, was a real autumn day. The ferry carrying me across to the other shore was empty. Unhurried, Verbin pulled on the cable with his paddle. I helped him. The surface of the water shivered with gray wavelets. The timbers of the ferry glistened, soaked by the drizzle. . . .

"One week more and I'll put it to bed," said Verbin, smiling, when the ferry came to a standstill beside the small wooden landing stage.

I picked up my little suitcase and stepped out onto the sand. Verbin followed me, lit a cigarette, and offered me one as well.

We talked about this and that. Already like two close relatives. He did not notice my emotion. Everyone thought I was going to Nerlug to sign on as an apprentice mechanic with a truck company.

It sounded very plausible. A typical career for a young fellow in our part of the world. But I was experiencing a strange emptiness beneath my heart, as I looked at the village, hidden behind a curtain of rain. I did not yet know that it was for the last time. . . .

Suddenly a female silhouette appeared in the hazy distance. A woman dressed in a long waterproof coat was walking on the beach at the edge of the water.

Verbin sighed. We exchanged looks.

"She still waits for him," he said softly, as if afraid that the woman on the opposite bank might hear him. "I saw him last winter, her husband. At Nerlug . . . Everyone knows he's alive. And she still hopes I'm going to bring him back to her one day on my ferry. . . ."

The ferryman was silent, his eyes fixed on the fragile silhouette, blurred by the rain. Then he gave me a look filled with a somewhat desperate jauntiness and spoke louder, in almost cheerful tones: "But you know, Dmitri, I sometimes tell myself that maybe she's happier than lots of others. . . . I've seen him, her man: fat, pompous. He looks like a Japanese oil magnate; he can't open his eyes, he's so bulging with fat. . . . But she's waiting for someone else, her young, lean soldier boy, with a shaven head and a faded tunic. That's what we were all like in the spring of '45. . . . Your aunt speaks the truth. It's why Vera doesn't grow old. Her hair's quite gray; you've seen her. But she's still got the face of a young girl. And she's still waiting for him, her soldier. . . ."

The few, rare passengers began to gather around the ferry. I shook Verbin's hand and set off along the rain-drenched road. . . . At the corner, when I had to leave the valley of the Olyei and enter the taiga, I glanced behind me. The ferry, a little square on the gray expanse of the waters, was already in the middle of the river.

I arrived in Leningrad after sixteen long days of traveling. Always in third class. Often without a ticket. Sleeping on luggage racks, dodging ticket inspectors, eating the free bread at station buffets. I crossed the empire from one end to the other — twelve thousand leagues. I crossed its giant rivers, the Lena, the Yenisey, the Ob, the Kama, the Volga. . . . I traveled through the Urals. I saw Novosibirsk, which seemed to me like Nerlug, only much bigger. I discovered Moscow, crushing, cyclopean, endless. But overall an Oriental city, and thus very close to my profoundly Asiatic nature.

Finally there was Leningrad, the only truly Western city in the empire. . . . I emerged onto the great square by the station. My eyes were heavy with sleep, but they opened wide. The apartment buildings had quite a different style here: packed close together, svelte and arrogant, overloaded with cornices, moldings, and pilasters, they formed long rows. This European rectitude, but above all the smell — a little acid, fresh, stimulating — fascinated me. I walked with a sleepwalker's tread across the square and suddenly uttered an "Oh!" which made all the passersby turn their heads. . . .

The Nevsky Prospekt in all its morning brilliance, veiled with a light-bluish mist, spread out before my astonished gaze. And at the very end of this luminous perspective, lined with sumptuous facades, shone the gilded spire of the Admiralty. I remained in ecstasy for several moments before the glitter of this golden sword pointing up into a sky that was slowly suffused with a pale Nordic sun. Through the mists that hovered over the Neva, the West was making its appearance.

In a blinding flash my gaze took in everything: the nostalgic charm of Olga's childhood as she walked, long ago, along the elegant streets of this city, to take the Saint Petersburg–Paris train with her parents; the noble soul of this ancient capital that would never become accustomed to the nickname its new masters had bestowed on it; and the shade of Raskolnikov, wandering somewhere in the depths of the foggy streets.

But most of all, I realized that in the midst of this scene tinged with autumn light, I would not have been excessively surprised to have run into Belmondo. In person. The one and only. His presence was becoming seriously conceivable. . . . I readjusted my knapsack and, with a resolute tread, made my way toward a streetcar stop. I did not know if this was the best means for traveling to my college. But the sound of their bells in the morning air was just too lovely. . . .

During my three years of studies, I had little news from Svetlaya. A few letters from my aunt, at first anxious and reproving, then calmer and filled with the details of a daily life that meant less and less to me. Absentmindedly, or quite simply so as to have something to say, she spoke in all her letters about the Olyei and the ferry: I was always watching Verbin repair the timbers or replace the cable. . . . "The saga of the old Chinese still continues," I said to myself, as I walked through the city of our Western dreams. . . .

There was also a card from Samurai. But it did not come from the village. It was, in fact, an amateur snapshot with a few sentences written on the back in a slightly distant tone. Evidently he could not forgive me for my flight, which he and Utkin considered to be a betrayal of our friendship. . . . Samurai reported Olga's death and told me that she had continued her evening readings right up to the last moment and regretted that "Don Juan" was no longer participating. . . . In the photo I was not at all surprised to see Samurai in the uniform of the marines on the deck of a ship. And hardly more so to see the white slabs of apartment buildings and the shadows of palm trees. The inscription in blue ink read: "The Port of Havana." I guessed that the deck of this ship represented a decisive step toward his boyhood project, his crazy dream that he had once told me about at Svetlaya, of joining the *guerrilleros* of Central America and rekindling the embers of the campaign of Che Guevara. . . .

As for Utkin, he never wrote to me from Svetlaya. But two years after my flight I saw a silhouette I instantly recognized in the dark corridor of our student residence hall. Limping, he came to meet me and offered me his hand. . . . We talked all night in the corridor, so as not to disturb the other three occupants of my room. Perched on the windowsill in front of the frost-covered glass, we talked as we drank cold tea. . . .

I learned that Utkin, too, had fled from Svetlaya. He had even succeeded in traveling farther than me, to the West, to Kiev. He was studying at the faculty of journalism and hoping one day to get down to writing "real literature," as he called it in a grave tone, lowering his eyes.

And it was in the course of that night that I learned in what circumstances Belmondo had finally left the Red October cinema and disappeared, maybe forever, from the corner of Lenin Avenue.

It was the winter following my flight. Samurai and Utkin were slipping along on their snowshoes through the taiga. It was engulfed in the half-light of the early hours of morning. They were going to Nerlug for the six-thirty performance. Without me. Another film they wanted to see again? Or perhaps so as to demonstrate — to whom? — that my betrayal did not affect their own relationship with Belmondo?

The cold was bitter, even for winter in our country. From time to time you could hear a long echoing sound like that of a gunshot. But this was tree trunks exploding, split open by frozen sap and resin. In weather like this, women in our village taking wash down from the clothesline would break it like glass. Truckdrivers would rage around tanks filled with white powder: frozen gasoline. And children would amuse themselves by spitting on the rock-hard road and hearing the tinkling of their spit as it turned into icicles. . . .

It was by the first rays of the sun that they saw it. On the fork formed by two thick branches of a pine tree. Samurai saw it first and had a moment of hesitation: should he point it out to Utkin? He knew his friend was going to be shocked by it. Always very protective of Utkin, Samurai had become even more so after my departure. So at first he wanted to walk past, as if there were nothing there. But in the absolute calm of the taiga Utkin must have sensed his hesitation, Samurai's intake of breath. He stopped in turn, looked up, and let out a cry. . . .

On the tree fork, hanging on to the rough trunk, his arms wrapped around it, was seated a man, his face white, covered in hoarfrost, his eyes wide open. His pose had the frightening fixity of death. His legs were not dangling but rigid in space, six feet above the ground. He seemed to be staring at them, directing a horrible rictus at them. The snow around the tree was churned up with the footprints of wolves.

Samurai studied the frozen face and was silent. Utkin, appalled by this encounter in the sleeping taiga, sought to cover up his dismay. He spoke quickly, volubly, trying to sound tough: "That must be an escaped political prisoner. Sure. I'll bet he's a dissident. Maybe he wrote anti-Soviet novels and they threw him into the Gulag, and then somebody helped him escape. Maybe he has manuscripts hidden on him. . . . Maybe he wanted — "

"Shut your trap, Duck," Samurai suddenly barked.

And with malevolent fury, speaking as he had never spoken to Utkin before, he went on: "Political prisoner! Gulag! Who are you kidding? The camp you can see from Svetlaya is a normal camp, Duck. You hear me? Normal! And there are normal men there. Normal guys who have simply stolen something or smashed someone's face in. And these normal guys play cards after work, in a normal way, write letters, or nap. And then these normal men choose their victim, generally a young guy who's lost at cards. You lost — now you have to pay. It's quite normal. And these normal men fuck him in the mouth and up the ass, the whole hut, each one in turn. So that instead of a mouth it's only beef hash, and between his legs it's mincemeat. And after that the poor guy becomes untouchable; he has to sleep next to the shit bucket; he can't drink from the tap the others use. But anyone can fuck him whenever he likes. And to escape that there's only one way: to throw himself on the barbed wire. Then the guard fires a few rounds into his head. Straight to heaven . . . That one must have got away when they were doing hard labor. . . ."

Utkin uttered a strange sound, between a groan and a protest.

"Shut your trap, I tell you," Samurai rebuked him again. "Shut your trap with your stupid fucker's romanticism! That's what normal life is, do you understand? Yes or no? Guys who come out after ten years of that life and live among us . . . And we're all like that, more or less. This normal life is how we live. No animal would live like that. . . ."

"But Olga, but Bel . . . Bel . . ." Utkin suddenly gasped in a tortured voice, without being able to continue.

Samurai said nothing. He looked around to mark the place well. Then he picked up his pike and motioned to Utkin to follow him. . . . They did not go to Nerlug that day. They missed their six-thirty rendezvous.

Later, sitting in the smoke-filled premises of the militia at Kazhdai, they spent a long time waiting for an official to be free to go with them to the site. Samurai was silent, shaking his head at intervals. His eyes were focused on invisible images of past days. Utkin watched these fleeting ghosts obliquely. He sensed that soon Samurai's voice would lighten, and in an embarrassed tone he would ask his forgiveness. . . .

Seated on the windowsill, that was how Utkin told me about the end of Belmondo's era in the land of our youth. . . . It was so strange to hear the sound of his voice in the corridor of our residence hall! His face was that of a young man with his first mustache, but through it shone the features of the injured child of the old days. The child who used to long so passionately for the start of adult life, hoping that he would experience love — like other people — in spite of everything. There was I, already cheerfully enjoying the love life of a carefree young male, and suddenly I perceived the infinite despair my friend carried within him. It was as if his face had been eroded by the indifference in women's eyes. By their blindness, so natural, so pitiless . . .

Utkin noticed the intensity of my stare. The shadow of a disillusioned smile flickered on his lips. He turned his head away toward the windowpane, outside which the chilly Leningrad night was turning pale.

"And when we came back to the place with the guys from the militia," he went on, "when we looked again at the escaped prisoner attached to his branch, I felt no more fear. No sadness or pain either. I'm ashamed to say it, but I experienced . . . a strange kind of happiness. You know. . . . I said to myself — in that language deep inside you that articulates things without using words — I said to myself that if the world's so horrible, it can't be real. And certainly not unique. That's it, I told myself. You can't take it seriously."

Watching the militiamen, assisted by Samurai, trying to haul the dead man out of the tree, Utkin experienced a mysterious revelation. This young prisoner, whose frozen fingers were now being wrenched open by the men, panting with their exertion, marked a certain limit. As did his own mutilated body? A limit of cruelty, of pain. A frontier . . .

The corpse finally yielded. The three militiamen and Samurai carried it toward the four-wheel-drive parked at the edge of the taiga. The prisoner's shapka fell from his head. It was Utkin who picked it up. He followed the others, at every step pointing his right shoulder up into the sky, as if he were trying to take a look beyond that frontier. . . .

We spent a whole day traipsing around the wet streets of Leningrad. We went into museums, crossed the Neva. I was proud to be showing Utkin the only Western city in the empire. But neither he nor

I was really in the mood for tourism. Even at the Hermitage we talked of other things. The previous night, Utkin had handed me three dozen typewritten pages — a fragment of his future novel. "In the tradition of *The Gulag Archipelago,*" he had explained. I was carrying them inside my jacket now; I felt like a real dissident.

Yes, even in the middle of the Imperial Palace we were speaking in low tones about the horrors of the regime. We criticized everything. We rejected the whole system. The Belmondo of our adolescence and his mythical Western World were transformed into an ideal of liberty, a plan of campaign. We still had a vision of the sun trapped in the barbed wire, impaled on the watchtowers. The gigantic pendulum must be activated! Time, our time, the dictatorship's unhappy victim, must be set free!

Our angry whispering threatened at any moment to erupt into a shout. Thanks to Utkin, it did.

"I've got nothing to lose! I shall fight, even in the camp!"

I started coughing, to cover up the echo of his words beneath the magnificent ceilings. The attendant gave us a suspicious look. We abandoned our regicidal planning session. There in front of us, beneath a red canopy, stood the imperial throne of the Romanovs. . . .

≋ 4 ≋

≈ 19 ≈

It is snowing on New York this evening. Or perhaps only on Brighton Beach, a Russian archipelago, where the white turbulence revives so many memories and inspires melancholy in the eyes of all those children of the defunct empire who end up here after arriving in the promised land.

We remain silent for a long moment as we walk along the boardwalk, beside the ocean. The smell of the wind — now a salt gust from the waves, now the piquant chill of the snowflakes — easily replaces words. The bitter cold of the night air evokes a whole sequence of past days that speak to us in profound, serious tones.

"I'm so sorry, but I just couldn't have come any earlier!" I finally say, in an effort to justify myself.

"It's all right. I understand!" Utkin hastens to reassure me. "When I saw him he was already breathing with difficulty; he could no longer speak. And yet when I looked into his eyes I had the feeling that he recognized me. . . . No, no. I don't think they could have done anything, even here. His body was riddled with steel. . . . Yes, I think Samurai recognized me."

He shows me a photo, brightly colored like a holiday snapshot. In front of the long mound of the grave, Utkin has been captured, involuntarily standing at attention. This is the Utkin of "twenty years later" with a little Trotsky-style goatee and eyes invisible behind his glasses. Beside him a woman crouches, seen from behind, piling up the earth around a plant with big purple flowers. Her very practical gestures make her astonishingly distant from, foreign to, the tortured gravity of Utkin's expression. . . .

So does everything come down to this little mound of fresh earth lost somewhere beneath the skies of Central America. . . ?

The dining room of the Russian restaurant, generally half empty, is well filled this evening. The Orthodox Easter. One can see the grizzled manes and noble brows of the first emigration, and some thin faces and embittered expressions from the latest wave; and plenty of Westerners, who have come to sample Slavic charm by candlelight. The musicians and the singer are not there at the moment — the obligatory intermission between two courses. Their repertoire matches the degree of intoxication. After the break come songs more in accord with the quantities of vodka consumed. Conversations become heated, remarks overlap, slowly spreading a confused hubbub across all the tables. And our host, the famous Sasha, like the conductor of an experimental orchestra, directs this cacophony, now coming over to this group, now to that one.

"Oh yes, Your Royal Highness. The only shashlik of this kind to be made in New York now is ours. After the death of Count Sheremetyev's chef. . . Yes, my good friend, this wine will help you forget your Moscow fallen into the hands of neo-Bolsheviks. . . . Yes, of course, madam, this follows a purely Russian tradition. And furthermore, you'll see that it will go perfectly with this slightly acid punch. . . ."

He seats us at one of the last free tables. I sit with my back to the room. Utkin stretches out his leg in the narrow space between the tables and lets himself down, facing me. The big mirror behind his chair transmits back to me the multicolored depths of the room filled with the vivid lights of the candles. On the walls hung with red velvet are the "icons" — pages from illustrated magazines cut out and stuck onto rectangles of plywood and covered in varnish. In one corner, on a cabinet, is a full-bellied samovar.

After the first vodka Utkin rummages in his great leather bag and brings out a colored volume reminiscent of a children's book.

"Since it's a time for confessions and faded dreams tonight . . ."

I open the volume, putting my glass aside. It is a comic book for adults. Quite "hard," from the look of it.

"These are my novels, Juan! Yes, all the plots are mine. The situations, the dialogue, the captions, everything. . . . Impressive, huh?"

I leaf through the colored pages. With some variations, the stories are all similar: the characters are clothed at the beginning, undressed at the end. The backdrop for their nakedness is sometimes a lush tropical wilderness, sometimes the luxurious interior of a villa, on occasion even the weightlessness of a spacecraft. . . . As the pages flick past, a whole firework display surges out of them: curvaceous backsides being grasped by the hands of hairy men; pink or tanned buttocks; genitals being flourished; hungry lips; luminous thighs. Suddenly I understand everything.

"So it was to write these that you made use of my love stories?"

Utkin looks sheepish. He pours us some vodka.

"Yes. But what could I do? You had so much experience. And I had to invent a new one every day!"

I turn over the very last pages of his book. I come upon a series of images that strike me as strangely familiar.

Utkin guesses what scene I have just discovered. He blushes, holds out his hand, and snatches the book from me, knocking over my glass. But I have time to take in the final sequence: the woman spread-eagled over the top of the grand piano, the man splitting her body in two and emitting roars in bubbles, like puffs of steam from a locomotive in a film cartoon. . . .

We mop up the vodka. Utkin stammers excuses. The waiter brings us borscht and sets a vessel of piping-hot buckwheat kasha beside our plates.

"So you see, I've sunk pretty low," says my childhood friend, with an embarrassed smile.

"Not at all. In any case, as you probably guessed, my princess was pure invention. I lied to you, Utkin. That whole story. It wasn't the Côte d'Azur: it was the Crimea, a hundred years ago, or a thousand years ago. I no longer remember. And she wasn't wearing an evening gown the way she is in your pictures, just a faded satin sundress. . . . Her body smelled of rocks baked in the hot sun. And as for the candelabra on the piano, I guess no one had lit the candles in them since the Revolution. . . ."

We fall silent and stir fresh cream into our borscht.

"It's stupid. I should never have shown you my masterpiece," he says finally.

"Of course you should. . . . Besides, the pictures are really good."

Utkin lowers his eyes. I see that my compliment has touched him.

"Thanks. . . . It's my wife who did those pictures."

"You're married? Why didn't you tell me?"

"Well, I did tell you about her once. . . . But we got married a month and a half ago. She's an American Indian. . . . And she's a bit like me. . . . That is to say — er — she's . . . she's a bit hunchbacked. She fell off a horse when she was little. . . . But she's very beautiful."

I nod my head with conviction, in a hurry to say something: "So you've found your Eurasian roots?"

"Yes. . . . Look, I think we're doing less harm with these comic strips than the people who sell all that kitsch that passes for literature in the States. . . . And what's more, if you noticed, in my strips the bodies are always beautiful. My wife wants them to be like that. . . ."

Utkin opens the book again above his plate and starts showing me the pictures.

"But the most important thing, you see, is that in each sequence there's a bit of horizon, a space, a panel of sky. . . ."

I can't help laughing. "Do you really think your readers have time to notice that bit of sky?"

Utkin is silent. The waiter removes our plates and sets the shashlik before us. We drink our vodka. Sunk in thought, my friend raises his eyebrows, his gaze lost in the bottom of his glass. Suddenly he proclaims: "You know, Juan, the Americans often remind me of monkeys playing with a clockwork toy. They press a button, the spring functions, the little plastic man starts turning somersaults. The object is achieved. . . . And it's the same in their culture. They construct a new genius and inflate him through TV, and nobody gives a shit about his books so long as the machine keeps working. Button — spring — and the little plastic man jumps around. Everyone's happy. It's very reassuring to be able to construct geniuses. With the help of the word . . . They juggle with ideas as old as the world, put them together in endless combinations, and sacrifice their own lives. Words, words, words . . ."

Utkin waves the empty bottle, signaling to the waiter.

"That's right. The life has gone, but the machine keeps

working!" he adds, fixing me with his tipsy prophet's eyes. "And it's a great division of labor, you see! The masses get sustenance from products like my comics and the elite from unreadable word puzzles. And you've seen how solemnly they hand out their literary prizes! It's like Brezhnev pinning a new gold star on some decrepit member of the Politburo. Everybody knows who's going to get the prize and why, but they go on playing at Politburos. It's the deathly ivy closing in on the West. The ivy of words that has killed life."

At this moment I see the musicians appearing in the mirror behind Utkin's head. The violin utters a light experimental groan; the guitar emits a long guttural sigh; the accordion fills its lungs, whispering melodiously. Finally, still in the smoky reflection of the mirror, I see her . . . *her.*

In her black dress, she looks like a long bird's feather. Her face is pale, without a touch of makeup put on for local color.

Now, this machine, I think to myself, is really working well. Sasha knows just the right moment to serve up the Slavic charm. . . . Their faces are softened by the abundance of food, their eyes misting over, their hearts melting. . . .

But the song which arises does not seem to be playing Sasha's game. At first it is a very soft note, which immediately tempers the bravura of the musicians. A sound that seems to come from very far away and does not succeed in dominating the noise from the diners' tables. And if this frail voice imposes itself a few moments later, it is because everyone, despite drunkenness and a full stomach, can sense those distant snows unfolding, beyond the walls hung with red velvet and the paper icons. The voice is slightly raised; now the diners cannot take their eyes off the pale face, with its gaze lost in the mists of those days evoked by the song. In the illusory depths of the mirror I can probably see her better than the others. Her body a long black plume; her face without makeup, defenseless. She sings as if for herself; for that cold April night; for someone invisible. The way a woman sang one evening in front of the fire in a snowbound izba . . . Everyone knows the words by heart. Yet we find our way into that distant night, lost in a snowstorm, not by deciphering the words but by staring at the candle flame until it starts to grow bigger, letting you enter its transparent aura. And the music becomes the cool air of the izba, which smells of a snow squall; the radiant warmth of the fire; the scent of burning cedar; the limpid silence of solitude. . . .

"That song," murmurs Utkin, "reminds me oddly of a story Samurai once told me. He was angry with himself for talking to me about the prisoners raped at the camp, and all that filth, even though I already knew about it. To him I was a child, and anyway, you know what Samurai was like. . . . When the militiamen had gone off with the frozen prisoner and left us alone, Samurai pointed to his nose. You remember that boxer's nose he had? He told me how it happened."

That day, a thousand years ago, Samurai had gone to sleep on the roof of an abandoned barn near Kazhdai. The ground was still white, but the roof, under the spring sun, was shedding its last patches of melting snow. It was a woman's voice coming up from below that woke him. He looked down from the roof and saw three men setting upon a woman. She was struggling, but feebly — in our part of the world, as she well knew, slipping a knife between someone's ribs is easily done. From their shouts Samurai understood that it was not exactly a rape: the men simply did not want to pay. Otherwise she would have had nothing against it. In a word, she resigned herself. . . . Samurai, tensed like a dog watching its prey, observed them. The men uncovered only the parts of her body they were going to use: they bared her belly, uncovered her breasts, seized her chin, her mouth — they were going to need that. And all this in a hurry, panting, with dirty little laughs. Up there on the roof, nine feet above them, he was seeing for the first time in his life how a woman's body is prepared for "that."

The woman, split in two, closed her eyes. So as not to see . . . Dumbfounded, Samurai repressed an "Oh!" The woman had dropped her heart in the snow. No, it was doubtless a simple handkerchief or some small purchase wrapped in pale paper. . . . It was a little pink parcel she was carrying in the inside pocket of the overcoat that the men had brutally ripped open at the collar. . . . But for a moment Samurai thought he had seen a heart plunging into the snow. He began shouting and slid down from the roof, his face tortured by the evil that filled his eyes. He raised his arm-swords in the air and brought them down on the heads and ribs of his enemies. He crumpled under blows from fists as heavy as clubs. Then he got up again, wresting himself away from the hands that were trying to hold him fast. Suddenly blood flooded the sky. Blinded, he slashed with his swords, sometimes striking air, sometimes human flesh. But the blood that filled his eyes was slowly dissolving the sticky clot of evil. . . . And when he was finally able to wipe his face with the sleeve of his jacket, he saw that the men were getting into a truck parked beside the road. And the woman, far away, very far away, was walking along beside the Olyei. . . .

I listen to his story, and I believe I can recognize the Utkin of the old days. His face lights up. He is a heavy, corpulent man, but his gestures are once more reminiscent of the thrusts of a wounded bird trying to take flight from the earth. And it is in his old tones, grave and sorrowful, that he confides to me: "That woman, she was the red-haired prostitute who used to wait for the Transsiberian every evening. You remember? . . . The one I wrote my first poems to . . ."

Utkin pours himself another glass, drinks it slowly. Has he even spoken? Or has that memory, buried beneath the snows, been born in my own fuddled head? And the blood flooding into Samurai's eyes, does it not have the warm smell of a forest in Central America? Samurai is stretched out at the foot of a tree, and what little vision he has left beneath the red flood conveys to him the image of two men in khaki approaching him cautiously. To finish him off. Yes, it is him that I see, his body riddled with metal, his smile defying the pain, true to the hero of our youth. To the one who taught us that bullets did not hurt and that death never came, so long as you looked it in the eye.

Stepping out of the heavy heat of the dining room, we pause for a moment on the boardwalk, before the somber expanse of the ocean. There is no light to be seen there. A dark infinity of water, snow, nothingness . . .

We end up at Georgi's, a tiny Georgian restaurant where life consists of long conversations with stray customers; views of the Black Sea on the walls; and the dreams of Kazbek, the old shepherd who welcomes us with his melancholy stare. Georgi greets us and brings us what he knows we need. Cognac, coffee, pieces of lime.

"In Tiflis a shell has destroyed my childhood home," he says softly, setting the bottle and the glasses on the table. "The world's going mad. . . ."

We remain silent. We are seeing ourselves as we were twenty years earlier in the midst of an endless snow-covered plain. . . . On the horizon the low sun of winter — that pendulum of history — was motionless, surrounded by watchtowers. . . . We had then spent several years of our lives, Utkin, I, and so many others, stirring things up around that disk stuck in the barbed wire: writing our subversive books, debating, demonstrating. We pushed against its inert bulk with our shoulders — with our words! Gradually the pendulum of history had begun to respond to our efforts. It was swinging more and more freely, and now its movement back and forth across the immense empire was becoming threatening. One day that giddy swing had dragged us in its wake, flinging us beyond the frontiers of the empire onto the shores of our mythical Western World. And it was from these lands that we watched the pendulum gone crazy — or finally free? — demolishing the very empire itself. . . . "And today, despite all my Western wisdom," I say to myself with a bitter smile, "I understand neither that frozen teardrop in the eye of the wolf they killed; nor the silent life beneath the bark of the ancient cedar tree that bears a great rusty nail in its trunk; nor the solitude of that red-haired woman, singing in front of the fire for someone invisible, in an izba entombed beneath the snow. . . ."

Utkin removes his glasses, and from the depths of his drunkenness he speaks slowly, focusing his blurred gaze on my face: "At the moment when I saw his name written in Roman script on the slab of his tomb — yes, his real name, not the 'Samurai' that we were so used to — well, at that moment I remembered everything. I remembered that day long ago, that walk with my grandfather on the banks of the Olyei. . . . There was a path in the snow there, you remember. A narrow furrow that ran along the high ground beside the shore . . . I often tormented my grandfather with the embarrassing question: 'What do you have to do to write?' Maybe more that day than usual. I had just read his story about the war. And the silence of the taiga was more mysterious than ever. He replied with jokes or grinned and changed the subject. Finally, unable to stand it any more, he swore an oath and pushed my shoulder, playfully of course. I was up on the ridge, just near the icy slope that led down to the shore. I lost my balance and began sliding at full speed down that smooth strip. The sky revolved in front of my eyes; the wall of the taiga tumbled on top of me; I couldn't tell which was up and which was down. My body no longer had any weight — my fall had been so precipitous but at the same time gentle. Above all, I had this new sensation. Someone had pushed me as an equal, without worrying about my lame leg! I ended up down below, buried in a mass of snow, amid some young pine trees. Dazzled and lighthearted, I looked around me. A few steps from my hillock, in the blue light of the winter evening, I saw them. . . . Naked. A man and a woman. They were standing, close together, thigh pressed against thigh, their bodies entwined. They were gazing into each other's eyes without speaking. A perfect silence reigned. The purple sky above them . . . The smell of the snow and the pine resin . . . My mute presence . . . And these two bodies of an almost unreal beauty . . . My grandfather called me from the top of the ridge. His words rang out, breaking the silence. The two lovers unclasped each other and fled toward the little bathhouse izba. . . . It was Samurai and a young woman I had never seen before and will never set eyes on again. As if she had been born in that moment of beauty and silence and vanished with it . . ."

Outside, the snow clings to our faces, reawakening feelings long since faded. Utkin turns up the collar of his overcoat to shield himself from the white flurries. His words mingle with the murmuring of the wind. I turn. Our footprints on the deserted boardwalk are reminiscent of those left by snowshoes along a railroad track in the midst of the taiga. As if Utkin were leading me toward a sleeping train on snow-covered rails . . . An empty coach, its windows covered in hoarfrost, is silently preparing for our nocturnal visit. Making ourselves at home in a dark compartment, we shall wait without stirring. He will come. He will walk up the corridor with his tired warrior's tread and appear in the doorway.

He will come! Weathered by the salt winds and the sun of all latitudes. Flushed with time tamed and space conquered. And he will call out in a voice still distant but smiling: "No. I haven't yet smoked my last cigar!"

And at that moment the train will slowly move off, and the stars of snow on the dark windows will leave increasingly oblique streaks. And in a long conversation that night we will learn her name, which cannot be spoken. She who was born one day in that moment of beauty and silence. Long ago by the river Amur.